The Make Or Break

By Ritsha Bernard

WELLREAD PUBLISHING HUB 2023

ISBN: 978-0-7961-0187-7

To:

My family, thank you for allowing me the creative space to work on this book. I could never express enough gratitude for putting up with my wild imagination and random ideas.

My friends who read my teenage fantasies and thought they were worth something, thank you for pulling me out of the shadows.

Everyone that helped in shaping this book to be what it is, God bless you.

Chapter 1

My feet remain in the same spot as I take in my surroundings. The earth's musky smell after the rain sprinkle makes me crave some soil. But now is not the time to start looking for a tree.

Maybe if I stand here long enough, this place will magically morph into something that doesn't make every part of me want to run after the bus I just got out of.

I sigh and stare blankly at the people that are being helped to carry their things from the side of Tuta Road to the corridors of a small block of shops. It's the only building around with a roof made of iron sheets and even those have seen better days.

"Hi," says a male voice next to me.

I didn't think anyone would be paying attention to me particularly. A good number of people got off the bus at this station and they've all been minding their business. I was more focused on ensuring that all my bags were removed from the boot than their faces myself. I've heard stories of how people have lost valuable items on such trips. My possessions may not be expensive but they are my current net worth.

"Hi," I reply without looking at the source of the voice. I'm blinking so hard to fight back tears that it will be a miracle if my eyelids don't fall off.

Maybe this is what depression feels like.

"First time?" he asks. The chuckle in his words is unmissable.

I nod, still not turning to look at him, "Just reporting." I have never felt so out of place in my life. Not even when I first stepped into the college premises and there was no one to direct me to the dean's office. I may have been younger then but I knew what to expect.

I've been apprehensive about this journey from the moment Precious sent me the photo of the list of successful applicants in the newspaper. My prayer had been to remain within the Western province. But such wishes are for fairy tales and rich people. In real life, you *go wherever your services are needed*. That's just a fancy way of saying 'You wanted a job so take it or leave it'.

I had never even heard of this district until I saw my name next to it. But a job is a job and to say I need this job is an understatement. I'm desperate for real income. If not for me then at least for my siblings' sake.

Precious was the one who made the application on my behalf as I did not live in Lusaka. She and I had hit it off since the first day we met in class at Natural Resources Development College. If kindred spirits exist, then she is mine. It's not an exaggeration when I say I couldn't have made it through college the same way had our paths not crossed.

We were together on the bus that has now disappeared out of my sight. Lucky for her, she gets to live in Samfya, the epitome of Luapula tourism. I'm happy for her but I'll be lying if I say that I don't feel a little envious. Ok, maybe a lot envious. My only consolation is that we are in the same province. Not that it makes a big difference. The distance and mode of transport between her town and mine don't look like a walk in the park from where I am standing.

My eyes are now trained on the dirt road in front of me. It is lined with grass-thatched houses, trees, and maize fields.

We were told while buying tickets yesterday that there is a mid-morning bus. But we thought it wise to get on the first bus. Especially in my case since I have to find connecting transport. I can't imagine being stranded in a new place at night.

This reminds me that I should get moving. The sky is clear but the rain pattern this year has been very tricky. I don't waste time on weather updates, I rely on what I see. Right now, all I see is a deceptive sun.

As if he has read my mind, the man next to me calls out to the boys that are watching us and looking to make some easy coins. The trio comes and carries my bags and his Addis storage box to the shops. He walks with me to the corridor and we sit on one of the small old benches, leaning against the wall. The water paint is so old it has accumulated enough oil from people's backs so I don't worry about it getting on my dress.

"Welcome to paradise," he says. "You're under which department?"

"Uhm, health. I'm a nutritionist."

"Oh, they have that position now? Interesting. I'm Wezi by the way."

"Sanana," I turn my head to look at him directly for the first time. He is wearing a dark hoodie and blue jeans. His skin is a couple of shades lighter than mine. He has a buzz cut and keeps a neat beard. Maybe just a few years older than me.

He is handsome but his looks are the last thing on my mind. I am alone in a place over a thousand kilometres from home.

This reminder stings.

A beat-up Canter pulls up in front of the shops and people rush to it to start negotiations with the driver.

Wezi doesn't flinch though.

I turn to him when the last piece of luggage is packed, "Shouldn't we be getting on board?"

This is stupid. I don't even know if this guy is headed to the same place I'm going.

"Don't worry, we have a lift," he smiles. "Your colleagues actually. They are in the field nearby. I just communicated with them and they should be here any time soon."

"Oh, thank you," I sigh. Free transport. All the way!

"Don't mention it. It's what works around here. You have to look out for who is going where and schedule your movements around that. It's something we all kind of get used to."

Sounds like a nightmare.

"Home is in Lusaka?" he asks.

"Mongu."

He whistles, "That must have been a hell of a journey."

"I had a bit of rest in Lusaka at my friend's place," I smile at the thought. This is probably my last happy memory.

"The one you sat with?"

He had noticed us.

"Yeah, she was posted to Lunga."

"Wow."

"But she will be based in Samfya, so that's better for her, I guess."

"Good for her. And you too, at least Samfya isn't so far from here."

I sigh and push away the twists of hair that are crowding my face, leaving only a few to hide my left eye a bit. I hope the concealer hasn't worn off. It's not that effective. I can't afford a good quality one yet. I should have listened to Precious when she suggested we both do braids, but I went for natural twists.

About fifteen minutes later, a Toyota Land Cruiser ambulance comes to a halt in front of us. We are the only ones left.

Wezi goes to talk to the driver and the two guys in the front passenger seats. They exchange greetings and he points towards me.

"This is one of your officers. She's just reporting," he says.

The three men step out of the vehicle and come to introduce themselves. The driver, an elderly burly man leads the way. The others must be in their late twenties or early thirties.

"Welcome, madam," the older man extends his hand. "I'm Katebe."

The two slim guys are Richard, the district information officer, and Mweemba, a clinical officer. Mr. Katebe jokes that I should ignore their advances.

The men put my large suitcase and two sack bags in the car.

Mweemba gives up his seat for me and joins Wezi at the back.

I jump into the car and take a long breath. I close my eyes and try not to pay attention to the bad road. I'm glad I didn't have to sit in the back of a canter in my dress. It's long enough, but still a dress. Dumb choice of attire for this trip.

We reach Milenge Boma slightly after 14:00. I'm so grateful because I don't even know where I'm going to sleep.

The structures in the boma are clustered together within the confines of the power lines. All the main buildings can be seen from one central place; the council offices, district administration block, district education board secretary's office, and district medical office are all a stone's throw from each other.

We drive straight to the district medical office block where Richard and Mweemba lead me to the planner's office. The district health director and the human resources officer are both not in the district. I introduce myself and hand the chubby man my appointment letter.

"Welcome, madam Yikona. I'm Mwila. We were not expecting you this soon," he says with a kind smile. "People like Mweemba here only showed up after they got their second pay."

Mweemba and Richard laugh.

"Do you know anyone here?" he continues.

"No," I clasp my shaking hands together in my lap.

He pauses for a moment. "Gentlemen, would you know if there is a vacant room at Mr. Mushili's lodge?"

The guys ponder over it then Mweemba says, "I'm not sure. There is a guy who just moved in. I think he works for the council."

"What about one of your girlfriends, Richard, they don't have a spare room?"

"Hmm boss, *yashani*? Me I'm a married man," Richard chuckles. "Mweemba is the one who knows a lot of single teachers."

Mweemba glares at his friend, "*Iwe*."

"Ahh," Mr. Mwila snaps his fingers. "Doesn't ba Katebe have some flats?"

"I doubt if those houses will ever finish. Even I have been waiting." Mweemba chuckles. "Let me ask him though. I'm sure he can know someone." He goes out of the room and returns with the driver.

Mr. Katebe explains that his second block of flats is not complete. He adds that one of his tenants, a female teacher who lives alone might be willing to accommodate me for the time being.

The four of us leave the office and get back in the car where Wezi has been waiting. We drive to a small complex of ten houses that, as I am told, were constructed for civil servants a little over a year ago. This is the first batch. The two-bedroom houses were ideally for the division two employees, but since the bigger houses are not yet in sight, the district administration decided to hand over these same ones to district department heads who had no accommodation. Only a few of the seniormost heads like the district commissioner, district doctor, and agricultural coordinator live in older, bigger houses. The council also has some houses for their workers, but generally, there is a big accommodation gap for the current workforce in the district.

Wezi lives in one of the houses in the complex, being the district works supervisor. He was the one who supervised the completion of the houses. We drop him off and proceed to do the same for Richard.

Mweemba lives on the other side of the boma near where they are taking me so he opts that they drop me off first.

If the lady agrees.

Chapter 2

We find the teacher whom Mr. Katebe had mentioned as Marjory outside her kitchen door.

She has just gotten home; a semi-detached flat with a roughcast wall.

"*Ba* Katebe, it's not yet month-end," Marjory giggles.

She's around my age.

Probably recently recruited as well.

"We have come for supper, and brought you a visitor," Mr. Katebe replies.

"Is that so?"

She looks over at me and waves her hand, "Hi."

"Hi." I hope my smile is better than my emotions right now.

Mweemba greets her with enthusiasm, but she mumbles a response without looking at him.

Mr. Katebe steps out of the vehicle and has a side conversation with Marjory. She looks over at me a couple of times as they speak. After a few minutes, she comes to the side of the car where I'm seated next to Mweemba.

"You can come in," she smiles.

Mweemba steps out to let me pass and we all go to the back of the ambulance to take out my stuff.

The men carry the heavier bags into the house.

"You are smart to arrive on a Friday," Marjory says when the two men have left. "I came on a Monday and had to report for work the following day. And that was before we even had electricity."

"Eish, I can imagine." At least she is friendly to me. I think about the hostile atmosphere between her and Mweemba but mind my business.

"Anyway, as Mr. Katebe told you, I'm Marjory. "I teach sciences at Milenge Secondary School. This is my second year in this god-forsaken place."

"That long?"

"I tell you. I can't wait to leave, not that it will happen any time soon. This place is like a toxic relationship. You hate it and then you get used to it, then you get bored and hate it again." She gets up and goes to pour water into the bucket with a heater element and switches it on. "You must be tired. Did you come with these guys from the junction?"

"Yeah, I was on the same bus with a guy called Wezi then he introduced me to them."

"Oh, so you met Wezi first. He's one of the few decent ones, at least from what I know. Small town," she adds when I look at her without saying anything. "You'll get used to knowing everyone's business because it just follows you even when you are minding your own."

I chuckle.

"Anyway, we can put your bags in there," she points to the room on the other side of the sitting room. "You can sleep in my bedroom tonight. I'll escort you to look for a mattress tomorrow then we can also see a carpenter about the bed. You'll need all the patience in the world though. I only had my bed made after six months of following it up."

"I don't even know how to thank you," I say with teary eyes.

I have no idea what I would have done if she had not taken me in.

"Oh, don't mention it. I was stranded when I got here. I wouldn't wish it on anyone. Is that your hair?"

"Yeah," I push away the twists of hair that are all over my face.

"Wow! Some of you have it all. I don't even know how many routines I have tried on this hair of mine," she laughs.

I can't tell how long her hair is. She has it in box braids that look like she wakes up extra early to style and gel around her edges.

She helps me drag my belongings to my assigned bedroom. She promises to clear out her things as soon as possible because she has been using the room as a closet, storage, and anything that requires dumping.

The house is a simple design; a kitchen that leads to a sitting room that separates the two bedrooms and a bathroom/toilet between the kitchen and the main bedroom. All the walls are painted with blue oil paint at the bottom and white water paint on the top part. Much like the walls of a school. There's no ceiling board, but luckily, the walls go all the way to the iron sheets. The tiny kitchen is neatly furnished with a wooden cabinet and a four-plate cooker. In the corner is an upright fridge.

I glance around the sitting room that has a three-piece set of black faux leather sofas, a small dining table, and a 32-inch TV on a wooden stand.

"What would you like to have for supper? I was just going to have some leftover rice and chicken. But there's sausage in the fridge," she offers.

"I think the rice will be fine. I bought some potatoes on the way, but I already had chips throughout the trip," I giggle.

"Well, you're the nutritionist, you know best. Maybe in time, I will learn to eat healthy too."

Marjory is a little shorter than me and very voluptuous. Her skin is a little lighter than mine. And her big brown eyes that she accentuates with dark eyeliner are her best feature in my books.

"Trust me, I'm the worst eater."

After supper I excuse myself to go and sleep while she watches a local series on TV.

I change into my night dress, remove the phone from the charger and reply to Precious' messages. My battery died just after I spoke with my mother upon my arrival.

Me: I'm alive

She replies almost immediately.

Precious: Finally! I thought you got lost, or worse.

Me: Lol. I arrived safely.

Me: Got a lift straight to the boma.

Precious: So where are you now?

Me: I've found someone to stay with.

Precious: Today? How?

Me: *Ala* the way God works, I'm still shocked. The driver of the ambulance I got on introduced me to his tenant who is a teacher and she has agreed to let me stay with her until I find my own place.

Precious: *Eh* shine. That's great.

Precious: Hope she's not dramatic.

Me: Lol no she doesn't look like that. She's as noisy as you though.

Me: And you? All settled?

Precious: This place also. I found no power and it just got back around 18. I'm at this *ka* lodge. It's not bad and quite affordable. The best part is that it's a walkable distance to and from the hospital.

Me: The same one you contacted?

Precious: No, the second one. That one was full.

Precious: And it would have been too expensive anyway. Those people don't even know the meaning of a discount.

Me: At least I'll only have to pay half the rent here. I'm just happy I have a place to sleep tonight.

Precious: Just finished unpacking. My tired is tired. But tomorrow I'm going to the beach. You can find love *ka*. Hahaha

Me: At least you're even thinking about love. *Kuno* I'm going to look for a mattress. Lol

Precious: *Iye*. At least I won't be stressing about that for now.

Me: I'm even sleepy.

Precious: Me too. Goodnight.

Me: Goodnight.

I don't know which side of the bed Marjory prefers. If it were my bed, I'd prefer the edge. I roll over to the wall and pray I don't have weird dreams.

On Saturday, we looked for the carpenter that had made Marjory's bed and negotiated a price for my single bed. Downpayment done, we went to the biggest general dealer shop in the district, which is no more than the size of a classroom. The owner is a retired head teacher. I didn't have enough money for the mattress that I wanted. Marjory vouched for me and I was able to get it on a part payment agreement.

Uncle Masiliso had only given me transport money. My pocket money is what I borrowed from my former boss who owns a chain of mobile money booths back home. I had only worked there for three months when I got the news of my appointment. I wasn't her favourite employee, but she came through when I needed it most. Even though I have to pay it back with interest.

This morning I made sure to be outside the human resources office at exactly 08:00, personal file in hand.

There are only male voices in the building. The one female around is the office orderly who merely greets me as she mops the corridor.

When the human resources officer has filed all my documents, he takes me around the building, introducing me to the other staff who welcome me. Some more warmly than others.

We meet the district health director just as we step outside the block. She is in the ambulance with Mr. Katebe, coming from her morning rounds at the hospital.

The human resources officer introduces me to the tall and curvy woman with long black hair that falls on her shoulders, nicely framing her beautiful oval face. The doctor tells me to go and see her when I'm done with the other departments.

I'm taken on another familiarisation tour to the district commissioner's office and the entire district administration block that houses most of the government departments. We proceed to the district education board secretary's office, and finally, the council block.

By the time I get back to Dr. Chisulo's office from the newly constructed district hospital, I have met so many people that their faces and names are all mixed up in my head.

Dr. Chisulo is in her mid-thirties. She has been in her position for almost a year. I instantly admire her boldness and the aura of authority that she carries. Heading an almost all-male department surely can't be a small feat.

"How are you settling in?" she asks, genuinely concerned. "Found a place to stay?"

"Yes, Mr. Katebe is the one who helped me." I clear my throat and try to maintain eye contact. "I'm squatting with one of his tenants at the moment."

It's a little intimidating just talking to her.

"Oh, that's wonderful. It's hard to find accommodation here, as you must have noticed. If I could house all of you, I would. And these guys just focused on building the hospital with zero consideration for staff houses. We are pushing for something. I hope it happens before we are all due for retirement.

"What's important is that you have a working space. You are here to serve the community regardless of your personal challenges," she says firmly. "You are going to be very busy. Richard has been handling some of your work so he will fill you in and you should figure out where to start from. You are the first actual nutritionist. That means you will have to brand your office from scratch and also learn a lot from everyone.

"You may be the technocrat, but the people with experience will teach you a lot more if you open yourself to learning. Ask as much as you can and also use your initiative where necessary."

"Yes, madam," I nod.

She looks at her watch and sighs, "Well, I have a meeting to attend. It's meeting after meeting for me. The accountant should be able to sort out your arrival advice and whatever allowances by the end of the day. My office is open to everyone. Let me know if you need my help with anything."

I excuse myself and go to the accountant's office. The man has a chip on his shoulder. He doesn't care that I have never filled in any documentation of this sort before.

After several spoilt forms, I finish all the paperwork and proceed to my assigned office at the hospital.

I spend the first week acquainting myself with the hospital environment, setting up my office with posters, files, and any relevant documents. Richard is very helpful in orienting me about everything I need. He is more than relieved to hand over to me. He runs me through the nutrition project baseline survey that they had just finished with WFP, adds me to the work WhatsApp groups, and gives me the contacts of key persons in various sections.

"Enjoy these days," he grins. "You will miss them soon."

"That doesn't sound very comforting," I giggle.

In the second week, I ask to go on two trips with the team that is conducting under-five community outreaches. I need to learn as much as possible if I am going to get some respect as well as develop good working relations. I don't want to be treated as an outcast in a work environment that doesn't have more people in my section of the department.

I'm fluent in Nyanja, but my Bemba is not as good.

I need to put more effort into learning before someone accuses me of saying what I didn't mean. Especially after being told that I will be involved in a lot of community interactions.

Marjory is helpful in that regard. She is not Bemba, but grew up in Luanshya so it came naturally to her.

The unnecessary attention is the one thing I have no control over. From both men and women. The men fancy anyone new in a skirt. The opposite is true for women. A new female is considered competition for the male population. You could easily be confronted for merely standing with someone's partner in public.

Marjory was right about other people's business finding you even when you are minding yours. I just entered a shop to buy a drink and the woman at the counter has run me through the life history of the man whom I met at the door on my way in. All I asked her was how she was doing.

I'm thrilled when I receive an email about a workshop. The project office is in Mansa, but all the implementing districts have been requested to meet in Samfya. The only thing on my mind is the famous beach. And the daily subsistence allowance of course. I could use any extra money. Especially since it will be coming almost at the same time as my first salary.

Seeing Precious will be the icing on the cake. I call her the minute I finish reading the memo. We agree to share her room at the lodge.

Chapter 3

The team opted that we start off very early on Monday even though Sunday was the check-in day. Dr. Chisulo, the district social welfare officer, Richard, and I leave Milenge at 04:00

This is the earliest I have woken up since I started work. I've been told that the district is very vast and sometimes I will have to go for field work before the break of dawn. I didn't think that would include workshops.

My efforts to finish off my sleep on the way prove futile due to the road. I've been thrown off my seat twice already.

We arrive in Samfya by 07:45 and go straight to the venue.

I catch a glimpse of the beautiful beach as I step out of the vehicle to climb the stairs up Chita Lodge.

The place is a beauty. I love the blend of modern architecture and the traditional feel.

My colleagues request Mr. Katebe to go and confirm their bookings in the various lodges they had contacted. I smile and tell him that I'm already sorted when he turns to me with a look of concern.

I take a couple of minutes in the conference ladies' room to fix my face and straighten my clothes. I unwrap the chitenge that I wore over my cotton pencil skirt. I had sworn not to wear dresses and skirts on trips after my arrival in Milenge, but I don't have office slacks yet and I couldn't wear jeans. I'd have to waste more time changing in case we arrived late.

Satisfied that my sky-blue shirt is not covered in dust, I make my way to the conference room.

The lodge staff members are finishing up the arrangements and putting bottles of water on the tables when we take our seats.

A nice-looking guy is setting up the projector with the help of a senior member of staff.

Some other teams enter and get settled.

I take out my phone to text Precious.

Me: *Iwe* **where are you? Even people from heaven have arrived.**

Precious: Running late. Long and annoying story. Keep a seat for me.

Me: Can't. We are sitting according to districts.

Precious: *Yaba.* **Be there soon.**

Me: Ok

Moments later, a middle-aged woman and man join the guy from earlier in the front seats. The guy from earlier announces that we will begin with a round of introductions. He says his name and that he is the project officer for Luapula province.

I stifle a giggle when Precious finally shows up, visibly embarrassed. I wave at her after she finds a seat next to one of her colleagues. She smiles back.

The first session goes by quickly.

Thankfully.

I'm famished by the time we have the mid-morning tea break. That is breakfast for most of us.

Precious and I don't get enough time of the fifteen minutes to get past greetings, but we have lunch and the rest of the week to catch up. Especially about the handsome project officer who keeps staring at her while she does everything to pretend as if she doesn't notice it.

Two group sessions later, we break off for the one-hour lunch at 13:00. Precious and I pick our orders and find a table in the far corner of the large dining room.

It's only been two weeks since we last saw each other. And even though we talk on the phone almost every day, there is still so much to catch up on.

I'm not sure what is tastier between the grilled chicken I'm dipping in the lemon and herb sauce or the direction our conversation has just taken.

"Wait, Musenge is *the* guy?" I have to put my appetite on hold for this.

"Yup," Precious replies, pretending to be casual.

"Oh, this is exciting!" I squeal, looking around to see if anyone is witnessing my childishness. "So, what are you going to do?"

"Nothing. What am I supposed to do?"

"This is fate," I put aside my knife and fork and tear apart the chicken drumstick and thigh with my hands then lick my fingers. I'm tired of pretending to be sophisticated.

Precious scoffs, "You read too many novels."

"Fiction is drawn from reality, just with better-looking men."

"With a lot of traumas."

"Everyone has trauma, babes. But that's not even the point. I saw how he kept stealing glances at you. And now it makes sense, he remembered you!"

The guy she had met at the beach three months ago during a trip with her sister turned out to be none other than Musenge, our project officer.

"Oh please, the guy was standing in front of the room. He was looking at everyone, including you."

"Not with the same intensity."

She rolls her eyes, "He probably has a girlfriend. I don't think the women in Mansa are not fighting over him. You know how eligible men are scarce in these areas."

"Tell me about it," I groan. "In Milenge, it's like everyone left a girlfriend or wife wherever they came from. They date women from there just so they can have someone cooking and washing for them, with some frequent sex. And those who didn't leave a wife or whatever, they want to sleep with anything that walks. Imagine a guy cheating on you with a *ka* grade twelve."

"Eww."

"You think that's bad? There's this guy at the hospital who was sleeping with two sisters. One had an abortion and the other one is hellbent on keeping the child."

"Wow. Your Zanis officers must be very occupied. I don't even know any drama here."

"You live in a lodge and your only routine is to and from work. Find friends, not that they should take my place, and live a little. We are stuck here until whenever."

"Hmm, two weeks in the village and you've already become a life coach," she grins.

"Speaking of men, you remember the guy I got off the bus with when we were coming?"

"There were a lot of men who got off the bus with you. Some even carried bales of sugar."

"But there was one, I think he had sat at the back. He was wearing a hoodie so, a bit tall, with a beard."

She has no idea.

I shake my head and continue, "Anyway, he is the district works supervisor. He is the one who even helped me get on the ambulance from the junction."

"Bring the juice," Precious beams.

I sigh, "Ah I don't even know."

"He's also dating other girls?"

"None that I know of. At least not within the district. He seems to be in his own world that one. My housemate said there was a girl that used to come in the early months that he moved there, but it's been a long time since she's seen her."

"Maybe they broke up."

I shrug.

"Plus, you would have the home advantage," she makes quotation marks around the last two words.

"I'm not that kind of person."

"Yet you're the one that's always talking about how *love is not scripted*."

Touché.

"Maybe you shouldn't listen to me all the time."

"So that's the only interesting guy in your whole district?" She sips on her juice.

"Nope, just the only one I like."

"Shit! Everyone has gone," she exclaims, looking around.

I look at the time on my phone and glare at her, "I rebuke this your spirit of being late."

She laughs.

We grab our purses and dash out of the dining room to rejoin the others for the afternoon session.

◆◆◆

Precious collapses on the bed when we finally get to the room. Today's meeting ended at 18:00 and we had to stick around the venue because it started raining a few minutes before closing.

"Here I was, thinking these workshops are a break from the office, *kanshi* it's even worse," she groans.

"Tell, me about it! My butt hurts. At least you even have a tarmac. I swear those potholes from home are not for pregnant people."

"Are you hungry? I can order for you."

"Hmm even if I like eating, after all those sandwiches and samosas?"

"*Awe*, I was just asking. *Kaili* this is heaven for you people from the village so I thought you'd want to eat all the nice food," she giggles.

"Heaven my foot."

"By the way, did you see *ba* Temwani's wedding?"

"I never liked *your* friend, we're not even friends on Facebook. She married that same guy?"

"Yes. It was on the Zambian Weddings and Kitchen Parties page."

"Good for her," I say, nonchalantly. The girl in question was our coursemate.

"Don't be a hater."

"There's a difference between being a hater and not caring."

She sighs, "At least she wasn't even your friend *friend*. *Ine* I never heard from her after contributing to the *ka* kitchen party. Some people are foolish *ai*."

"Serves you right," I laugh. "Someone only remembers you when it's convenient and you go all out for them."

"Says the girl who couldn't tell that her *boyfriend* was stringing her along for two years. Where did you even get the courage to dump that bum? The way you used to go and cook as if it was exam practicals."

I take off my dress and grab a towel, "I don't want to talk about useless things."

Chapter 4

My dreams of lying on the beach will have to be put on hold because we were always finishing up late in the evening. I barely even set foot on the sand the afternoon that Precious dragged me to go and take pictures.

Dr. Chisulo communicated last evening that we would be leaving very early in the morning. We have to go to Mansa to pick up a few things for the hospital. She said I could meet them later at Musaila junction if I wanted, but I opted to go with them. Musaila is about ten kilometres from Samfya town on the main road leading to Mansa and connects to the other road going to Milenge. I wasn't going to pass on the free transport to Shoprite. Just thinking of another calculated trip makes me cringe. It takes two days for a round trip and there is no bank in our district.

I text Marjory to ask what I can get for the house. She rarely travels during the school term and unlike her, I have more access to free transport and more work trips going forward. I will always be indebted to her for taking me in and letting me use all her things while I settle in properly. Such kindness from people you just meet is uncommon.

My district is among the first five that will be implementing the nutrition project in the province. That means household surveys and everything related.

Mr. Katebe picks me up from the lodge at 07:00 and we follow the others to their respective lodges.

We reach Mansa town less than an hour later and proceed to the provincial medical office.

After brief introductions with the senior staff that are in the office, Dr. Chisulo excuses me.

I go on a mini tour into town, getting some dry relish from the market and meats from Zambeef. I deposit some money into my mobile money account and send one thousand kwacha to my mother. I get a taxi and head to Shoprite.

I start with a cooler box and other bigger and more important items then move to the junk food section. Being a nutritionist does not exactly put me above bad eating habits.

It's only one life. A little treat won't hurt.

By the time everyone else makes their way to Shoprite, I am done with all my shopping.

With my fresh foods in the cooler box, two Rambo plastics, and a bag of potatoes at my feet, I wave at Mr. Katebe. He has parked opposite the supermarket entrance, some metres away from where I'm standing. He strides over and helps me carry the groceries to the car.

"So now I can come for supper," he says.

I giggle.

Just as we finish putting my things beside the ambulance, Wezi gets out of the taxi that is now parked next to us.

"Big man," Wezi says to Mr. Katebe.

"Co-pilot," the older man replies with a grin and goes to fist-bump him.

The two seem to have a fond relationship. Mr. Katebe, as I have come to know him, is a no-nonsense, but kind and funny man. He has two wives.

Wezi gestures to the taxi driver to help him take out his luggage; a storage box.

"What have you brought for us?" Mr. Katebe asks him, moving the box to where my cooler box is.

"Just the usual."

Wezi smiles at me and we exchange greetings. I've only seen him a few times from afar since the day we first met. He was not even in his office when I had been taken for official introductions.

Mr. Katebe opens the back doors of the ambulance. He moves the medical supplies boxes to one side, takes out the folded wheelchair, and asks Wezi to help him tie it up on top of the vehicle.

When everyone else is done with their errands and their things neatly packed in the car, we leave for Milenge.

The doctor and the district social welfare officer are seated in front. Richard, Wezi, myself, and another guy who had joined us in Mansa are in the back, 'face your enemy' style.

Wezi is sitting next to me.

We make a quick stop to pick up two more health staff who are going to some rural health posts along the way.

When Richard starts saying something to Wezi, I take out my phone and text Precious.

Me: Leaving Mansa now. And guess what, *ba* works supervisor is in the cruiser with us, sitting next to me! He was coming from Kitwe.

Precious replies with bell emojis.

I shake my head and put the phone on my lap.

Wezi sees me smiling to myself.

"How was your first workshop?"

"It was all right," I don't want to sound too excited. "A little too busy, but ok."

"Did you like the beach? It's been years since I went there."

"Loved it, didn't spend a lot of time on it though, the meetings always ended late. I'll have to make a personal trip there to just relax. My best friend lives in Samfya."

"The one you were with on the bus."

"Yeah," I smile to myself.

He *still* remembers.

The rest of the journey is mostly quiet. Everyone looks exhausted and eager to get home.

We drop off Dr. Chisulo first, then the lady from social welfare, and Wezi and Richard.

Marjory is waiting for me outside our house.

"*Ba* landlord," she says to Mr. Katebe.

"*Ba* tenant," Mr. Katebe smiles back.

She and I carry the groceries inside the house.

Chapter 5

I left home with only one goal in mind today; to wind up my project community awareness activities and go bac k home to sleep the whole weekend away.

But as they say, what comes does not beat the drum.

When we get on the road that leads to the school where we are going, we discover that the bridge connecting to the other side had collapsed due to the heavy rains last night. It will take at least a week for the Zambia National Service team to fix it.

We do not have a week. This must be concluded as soon as possible so that I submit the report and move to the next stage.

The only alternative is to cycle for at least three kilometres and then canoe across the lagoon that separates the community from where we are.

Mweemba borrows a bicycle from one of the locals working on the bridge. I jump on the carrier and the two of us soldier on.

Mr. Katebe remains behind with the vehicle.

Two women are about to paddle to the other side of the lagoon when we get to the harbour of one old canoe. We join them.

I regret my decision the minute we start moving. The canoe is only wide enough to accommodate you if you squat or kneel and hold the sides. The two-hundred-metre distance feels like an eternity.

By the time we get to the other side, I have recited every memory verse and prayer I know. I jump out of the canoe as soon as it hits the hard surface. We walk a good five hundred metres before getting to the school where our meeting is to take place.

As if our taste of Noah's era is not enough, we have to settle the squabbles that arise among the people we find. Some of the villages that are not in the communities selected for the first phase of the survey have shown up to the meeting, demanding to be included.

I'm still learning how to deal with such situations so I let Mweemba handle most of the bickering while I provide the information we are here to deliver.

It is 17:00 when we conclude the meeting, followed by threats to be reported to the area member of parliament by those who still feel aggrieved.

I cannot bear the thought of getting back in that canoe that's triggering the claustrophobia that I have just developed. Even though it's the shortest route to where we left the vehicle.

Luckily, one of the teachers at the school who was also present during the meeting has a car. He offers to drive us up to the bridge. I cannot even begin to express my gratitude.

Our luck is short-lived.

While Mr. Katebe had been trying to reverse the vehicle after we had left, one of the tyres slipped into the edge of the swampy road. He had been stuck there for hours and there was no network. There are no trees to which he could tie the winch and it is risky to push because the space in the sides is too narrow for the land cruiser to reverse. It is water and soft ground everywhere.

One of the locals gives us directions to where the Zambia National Service team is camped with their machinery. Mweemba and I get back into the vehicle and it takes us thirty minutes to get to the camp. It's now past 19:00.

The tough-looking officer in charge simply tells us that there is nothing they can do about our situation at this hour.

I walk back to the car with silent sobs. I did not carry anything else apart from my water and snacks, not even a warm enough coat. This was supposed to be a day trip!

The teacher drives us back to his house. He offers us supper and a place to sleep.

The meal is Nshima and some plain fried eggs which I down quietly. It's rude to show disdain for something people are doing for you as a favour, but If I sit here any minute longer, I might start crying. Ugly, top of my voice crying.

I excuse myself and go to the spare bedroom I have been assigned for the night. Mweemba takes the small sitting room sofa. He has tried to cheer me up, but my sense of humour is on a break right now.

I've never been bitten by so many mosquitos in my life. By 03:00 I run out of sleep and spend the rest of the night counting the stars from the small wooden window. My phone battery is dead and my USB cable is back in the ambulance.

As I watch the break of dawn, there is no doubt in my mind that this experience will be the first one I tell everyone who ever asks me about my life in Milenge.

The national service bulldozer has already pulled the ambulance when we get to the bridge. They have also diverted the flow of water and put a temporary narrow bridge made of logs for pedestrians.

Mr. Katebe is smiling as he watches me get in the car.

I'm itchy everywhere and the swellings from the mosquito bites keep getting bigger.

"How was your first night in the field, madam?"

I shake my head, "*Ba* Katebe, let's just go."

He and Mweemba reminisce about the countless times they have been in similar situations on our drive back home.

Never again in my life will I ever go for field work without my toiletry bag and a change of clothes. It doesn't matter if it's just behind the office.

I'm going to buy a power bank or two. And a smaller phone for use in the field because it seems the network out here is not compatible with smartphones. I'm also going to be grateful to be eating any kind of relish as long as it has tomato in it, especially eggs. Even though I hate eggs fried in tomato soup.

Chapter 6

My list of enumerators is almost complete. I need twenty in total. The email came in yesterday and I have to submit the names before I knock off today. I spent the whole morning moving from department to department.

I'll be damned if I haven't shed off at least a kilo by now.

I don't know a lot of people yet so I'm heavily depending on recommendations from department heads.

Richard, who is among the enumerators by default, says he is leaving it up to me to deal with that. He doesn't want people following him around. He claims that since I'm new, many officers will shy away from confronting me about being left out. He only asked that I include one of our two registry clerks per phase. The first phase of enumeration is in April and the second will be in August.

I have five enumerators from our department, myself included. I've sent out letters requesting one officer from the smaller departments. There are three camp officers from the Department of Agriculture and two from Community Development. The district commissioner has submitted two names. I need some from education too.

I make a call to Marjory to ask if she is done with her classes. She says she's on her way home but can come to the hospital.

"I don't know what's worse between the smell of antiseptics and the medicines in this place," she says after taking her seat in front of me.

"You should just be bathing," I giggle.

"*Enhe*, what were you saying? I just heard *money* and I already started making a budget on my way here."

"When are you closing?"

"Next week Friday."

The training is on the Monday after.

"I've been told to submit a list of enumerators for the household survey. I wanted to add you if you are not going home for the holidays."

"Going where? *Iwe*, this is money we are talking about. I can even miss my own wedding."

"Today you don't want to go and meet your boyfriend?"

"My friend, men come and go. Money is the only thing that will never stress you."

"Anyway, it's for a month."

"Hey! 30 days? Allowance?"

I nod.

"And you are wasting time asking me? You don't know my last name?"

"Eh, I didn't want to impose. Maybe you hate—"

"Just put my details *uko* not *ifyama* maybe."

She helps me verify the names of three other members of staff under the district education office.

"Now how to get permission from my head of department," she sighs.

"But you will be on holiday," I frown.

"We still have to get permission, just in case we are needed for something. *Elo* that *ka* short man hates me because I'm more qualified. He thinks I'm there to take his job."

"Leave that to me."

When I see her off, I finish up the list, print the names and go to the education offices. The board secretary happens to be out of the district, so I proceed to Mr. Mushili, the District Education Standards Officer. His name is on the list and I ask him to confirm the availability of the other officers. He gives me the go-ahead.

I later go to see the head of the sciences department at Marjory's school. We have a small chat. I pretend to be interested in whatever he is on about, then present him the request letter signed by Mr. Mushili. I explain that those are the officers that have been approved by the board secretary.

He is not going to overrule that. Mr. Mushili is even more revered than his superior.

◆◆◆

The intensive five-day training is held in Mansa. Precious and I don't see each other as we are being trained in separate cohorts. Her district is in the next batch.

The training venue is Mansa Hotel, but Marjory and I are sharing a room at Central Inn Lodge where most of the participants have opted to be accommodated. It is more affordable, closer to town, and more importantly, closer to Shoprite. It's easier to grab breakfast and snacks on our way to and from the meetings.

Marjory insisted that we have supper at a restaurant near the lodge today. Someone had told us that they make some *nice* pizza. It looks relatively new. Or maybe the owner doesn't care that much about interior appearance.

We take one of the plastic tables in the centre.

"Will your people give us these fancy tablets to keep when this enumeration thing is over?" Marjory says, scrutinising her tablet while we wait for our order.

"Just buy a new phone *mami*," I chuckle.

"Ah *iwe*, but these will just be wasting away in your office."

"It's not a one-time thing. We will be retargeting every year."

"Even more reason! *Elo,* it has a nice camera," she takes some selfies of the two of us and bows her head to scroll through them. "This was a good one. Now I have to ruin it by cropping out that man."

"Just put an emoji when posting."

"Hell no, he just won't make it to my wall. You want people to think he is the one who brought us here."

"How?"

"He's smiling. Who even smiles in a stranger's photo? He doesn't even look like he can buy us the pizza."

"Don't put nudes in that phone even. You will scare away the donors," I giggle.

"Reminds me of a friend who claims that it was her child who accidentally posted a video *mu* work group," she breaks into a roar of laughter.

"Of herself?" I stare at her wide-eyed.

"No, just these same trending ones that people circulate."

"I would die. Why do people even keep these things?"

"Would you take one for your partner though?" she grins.

"No way. If someone wants to see these stretchmarks, they'll see them in person."

"Now if it's a long-distance relationship or they are out for work for some time?"

"Nope," I take a sip of my juice.

"Video call?"

"Especially that! What if you break up and the person decides to embarrass you?"

"*Ninshi* they also send *weh*. How dumb do you have to be to not have your own blackmail?"

"So how many people have you sent to?"

"Who said anything about me sending?" she smirks and brings the straw of her drink to her lips.

A waitress brings us our large-size pizza. Marjory takes a glance at the thin pastry with scattered tiny beef toppings and cheese that looks like it forced its way there. She looks up at me with her mouth open. I close my eyes and bring my hand to my mouth as I struggle to hold back the roar of laughter threatening to burst from my throat.

◆ ◆ ◆

We had agreed to wake up after 09:00, but I forgot to change the alarm time. It's 09:00 and we've been awake for the last two hours.

"*Ala* you just don't know what you have done," Marjory says, shoving the last of her clothes in her bag. She prefers to pack everything at the last minute. "I've never been involved in anything like this. So, if I hadn't welcomed you that day, I would have never had such an opportunity."

I shrug, "Maybe that's how God works."

"*Awe* sure it can only be God, *pantu* these things don't just happen. Is it still karma if it's something good?"

"You've started. Have you removed your pants from the bathroom?"

"Shit, I almost forgot," she rushes to the bathroom and gets back in a couple of seconds. "I've heard stories of people using pants for rituals and whatever."

"You've spent too much time around superstitious people," I chuckle.

"Ok you leave yours we see."

"I'm not giving up a pant I just bought for your silly theories."

We leave our bags at the reception and head over to Shoprite to buy groceries and some necessities for the fieldwork.

"You should also get gum boots," I say to Marjory, who has just thrown a mosquito repellent spray bottle in the trolley. We are moving to the cereals section. The supermarket is full of people and some shelves are already empty.

"Hmm, that's exaggerating now," she giggles.

"Oho, have you gone to any place in the district apart from the boma? Wait until the car gets stuck and you have to step in the mud to push. Or you get whipped by shrubs on the bicycle or motorbike."

"You make it sound like a horror movie."

"Welcome to my life."

"Fine!" she rolls her eyes. "Do I need an astronaut suit too?"

"No. Just a shield and an assegai."

We make contributions for fuel and Mr. Mushili drives us and two others back to the district in his car.

◆ ◆ ◆

When I have confirmed that everyone has their tablets and lists of names, we all get into our respective vehicles. I managed to borrow two land cruisers from other departments. Each one of us has been assigned four communities. We will be dropped off at our first points until it is time to move to the next and so on.

Marjory and I get in the same vehicle. She is among the five officers on my team. We drop her at her first station fifty kilometres from the boma. My community will be the second last drop-off.

Richard and Mweemba are leading the two teams that have gone in the other directions.

After six hours of dirt roads, makeshift bridges, and sparse villages, we finally reach my first community which is along the boundary between Milenge and Chembe. The *school* where I am to stay for the next couple of days is nothing but rudimentary walls partitioned into three rooms. The iron sheets had been blown off by a recent storm and one side of the wall collapsed a few days ago.

The sole teacher at the school and his wife welcome me into their home. It's not that big, but has three bedrooms. They let me have their girls' bedroom for the rest of my stay.

It hasn't even been a week and I already wish we had done so many things differently. I'm beyond stressed out, but I take my mistakes as lessons and hang on. There's no need to break down now when I'm the one primarily responsible for all this.

Some of the villages are as far as fifteen kilometres from the school, which is my starting point. I'm paying a reliable committee member to take me to the places I can't walk to with his bicycle. My behind hurts from all the hours of sitting on the carrier and my experience in cycling does not include snake paths.

Thank God for gumboots because the shrubs that are thrashing my legs would have caused serious bruises.

I don't remember ever being so glad to see anyone in my life as I am when Mr. Katebe drives up to the tiny classroom block. I've been sitting here for hours waiting for him. I would have hugged him if it wouldn't be so weird. The last four days have been a crazy episode of the Survivor series.

I almost forget to bid farewell to the two women that have been keeping me company in the dilapidated classroom with only three desks.

This joy is short-lived when he drops me off at the next point and it will be another three or four days before I hear the sound of a vehicle.

What bothers me most about these distances is that it takes more than two hours for some children to walk to school. My emotions don't matter though. I could get attached all I want, but I can't change the situation. My job is to conduct interviews about nutrition levels. Not to overhaul practices embedded in cultural history.

The exhaustion and a piriton pill help shorten the nights. I haven't experienced superstitious dreams or anything of that sort, but still, I just want to get back to my bed. The boma now feels like the best place in the world.

Mweemba's last community was closer to mine so instead of waiting for his vehicle, we picked him up. We are on our way to our third communities when Mr. Katebe brings the car to an abrupt halt. A middle-aged man is pushing an old bicycle with a heavily pregnant girl who can't be older than sixteen on the carrier. An older woman stands on the other side of the car.

The pregnant girl is in pain.

Mweemba immediately gets out and swings into action. He and Mr. Katebe aid the females to get into the ambulance. The man says he will meet them at the health post because there is nowhere to put the bicycle.

Mweemba sits with the women in the back as we drive off. I hate speeding in these terrains, but we are now in emergency mode. The health post where they are going is ten kilometres ahead of us.

We only drive half the distance when Mweemba bangs on the glass. Mr. Katebe stops the car.

The girl has gone into labour. They have to do it now.

This is the first time I'm close to anyone delivering a baby. Mr. Katebe goes behind to work with Mweemba. I remain in my seat, covering my ears to block out the girl's terrifying screams.

My whole body is shaking when he comes back to start the vehicle.

We arrive at the health post where the health staff put the women in a small ward and clean up the baby properly.

When I get a bit of composure, I walk over to the girl and give her the chitenge that I was wearing and a hundred kwacha to buy some soap. Other than the handbag that the older woman is holding, nothing is indicating their preparedness for this baby's arrival.

The mother of the girl thanks me and asks me to give the child a name. I name her Sepo, explaining that it means hope in my language.

My hands are still shaky when I open the car door and scoot to the middle seat.

None of us speaks about the incident on our drive.

I spend my birthday in the field because I have a call back in one of the communities. The time I was supposed to enumerate some households in a section, there was a funeral. Breathing a sigh of relief, I shut my eyes on the drive back to the boma. I'm finally done with the first phase of enumeration after almost five excruciating weeks. The only things on my mind are a long hot bath and an even hotter cup of drinking chocolate.

There's been some normalcy in my life after the survey. I'm waiting for the final list of qualifying households to be sent so that we proceed to distributions. My normalcy is dealing with malnourished children and mothers at the hospital and neighbouring clinics from morning to 17:00. I love the small difference that I'm making. But I'm beginning to question if that's also making me immune to the sound of people's cries. I used to wonder how doctors managed to be calm in life-threatening situations and hold stoic expressions when delivering even the most heartbreaking news. I think I get it now.

Marjory only had early morning classes today. She texted that she would cook Nshima for lunch. We usually have leftover relish and whoever gets home early cooks whatever else is needed.

She's almost done with the cooking when I get home.

"Are you going back to work?" I pour some water into a glass from the dispenser and take a long gulp.

"Unfortunately. I'm on duty."

"Aargh. Adulting is a scam."

"I tell you. These kids can send you to an early grave if you are not strong." She stops stirring the pot of Nshima and turns to face me, "I thought primary school pupils were a handful, but no, these *ku* secondary are the worst. Imagine this one asked me out of nowhere *ati* 'Madam, since the Bible tells us not to have sex until marriage, why do we have sexual urges in puberty according to biology?' Who even comes up with such thoughts?"

"Now that I think about it," I tap my chin. "Why don't we receive these feelings on our wedding day, madam teacher?

"Oh, shut up," she scoffs and turns back to the stove. "Some of these pupils have too much life experience. The other day I found one of them calling the friend by her child's name."

I burst into laughter, "I can't even call my sister that. It's like dignifying the situation. And if I have kids, stick to using my government name."

"You're just saying that. You're the same people who first obsess over the title of Mrs."

"It can never be me. Remember that friend of yours who kept referring to herself as *Mrs* during the workshop?" I laugh.

"*Iye* it's like she can't believe the husband is hers."

"If you start that behaviour with me, I'm ending this friendship."

"Maybe you even have a higher chance of getting married first," she grins.

"It doesn't matter. I'm Sanana before anything else."

I carry my plate of food to the dining table. Marjory always cooks very soft Nshima for lunch claiming it doesn't make her drowsy compared to the hard one. I never experience the difference.

Chapter 7

The nutrition committee members help me pack up at the end of our discussion. Some of the women stay behind to keep me company as I wait for Mr. Katebe to pick me up.

I needed to conduct some monitoring. Since all our departmental vehicles are busy with child health week activities, I scheduled my programme around their timetable.

The community I'm visiting today is just 15 kilometres from the boma. But it will be a couple of hours before they come to pick me up as they have gone further into the outskirts.

The women and I are on the waiting bench outside the rural health centre. One of them who lives nearby offered us a gourd which we are sharing. They are asking me personal questions. I am telling them half-truths as we watch the men constructing a maternity ward on one end of the building.

I hadn't noticed during the meeting that Wezi had come here to check on the construction works. I heard the motorbike, but I assumed it was one of the health centre staff.

The wind outside is unforgiving, but there are too many crying babies inside and my ears have had just about enough of it.

Wezi comes over to where I am.

He is wearing a dark blue reflective work suit and safety boots. I'm not sure if it's just me or if he looks hot in the attire.

"Hi," he smiles.

"Hi, how are you?" I try to be casual.

It's been weeks since I last saw him. Not that I actively make efforts to see him. It's just that this is a small town. If I can frequently run into faces I don't like, it should be possible to also run into him from time to time.

"I'm good. Just came for some inspections. But I'm done now and about to head back."

"Oh, that's nice."

Where has the confidence I had not so long ago gone all of a sudden?

The ladies say their goodbyes and it's now just the two of us on the bench.

An awkward moment passes.

"Are you done with your activities?" he turns to me.

"Yeah. Just waiting for these guys to pick me."

"Great. Used to the fieldwork yet?" he grins.

I sigh, "*Used* sounds like a bit of a stretch for me. Are *you* used?"

"I try to pretend that every day is my first time. It helps to keep the spirits high."

"I think I'll try that attitude," I smile.

"I can give you a lift back to the boma if you want," he says, getting up.

I think about it for a second.

I'm shivering from not having worn a warm enough coat and my mineral water is almost finished. It's past 13:00 and I don't know how much longer it will take for the others to come for me. The timeframe for their outreaches depends on the community turnout.

"I've never been on a motorbike before," I finally say, standing up.

He raises an eyebrow, "All this time? You could have even learned how to ride one by now."

"Pass," I giggle.

The week I reported was when the forestry officer who had broken his leg after falling off his motorbike was admitted. I lost all the will to ever learn how to ride one that very instant. My office even has a designated motorbike, but it is Mweemba who usually uses it.

"I actually learned how to ride from here."

"Nice."

Again, pass.

I inform one of the health workers that I'm leaving and ask them to pass on the message to Mr. Katebe when he comes. I can't get through to him.

"How do I balance?" I ask Wezi while taking my seat behind him on the Bushlander. He has given me his helmet. I fumble with it for a minute before managing to fasten the buckle under my chin.

"Just hold that metallic thing behind you tightly. And whatever happens, keep your feet on the foot-pegs."

It's only 15 kilometres, I tell myself.

I can be brave for 15 kilometres.

He starts the engine and turns the bike around in the direction we are going.

We hit a small bump and I throw my arms around his waist, hanging on for dear life.

His body tenses and he lets out a chuckle.

I don't care though.

I have only one life and I am not losing it in Milenge, on this motorbike.

I hold on to him tightly all the way up to my yard.

"Thank you very much," I say, handing him back the helmet when I get off the bike.

"You're welcome," he nods with a smile.

I walk into the house and find Marjory standing by the kitchen sink. She has a big smirk on her face. She had been peeping through the window.

"You're now even catching rides *ka*."

I roll my eyes and walk past her, "Don't start. We just happened to be in the same place at the same time."

"Same place at the same time huh? First, it was at the junction, then Mansa, and now in the field. Sounds like a love story waiting to happen."

"We live in the same district. We are bound to bump into each other."

"I've never bumped into him like that," she follows me up to my bedroom door.

"I'm sure you have lesson plans to make," I turn around and close the door with a grin.

She goes away singing Shekhinah's *Suited*.

Two days after Wezi dropped me off, I receive a text around 19:00. I swallow the mouthful of chips and push aside my half-empty plate. I grab the phone from the dining table to check who it is, hoping it's not work-related.

Unknown: Hi

Me: Hello

Unknown: Wezi here.

I sigh and try to compose myself. I quickly save his number before replying.

Me: From where? ☺

Wezi: Hahahaha. How are you?

Me: I'm good. You?

Wezi: Can't complain. How was work?

Me: All good. Yours?

It wasn't. But I don't know him well enough to vent about the accountant. And the women that can't be bothered to follow instructions concerning their own children's health.

I don't want him to think I whine about my job.

Something about first impressions.

Wezi: Nothing to write home about. Lol

Me: Lol

Wezi: Watchu up to?

Me: Just finished having supper.

Wezi: What were you having?

Me: Potato salad and grilled sausage. I hate fried sausage.

I don't even know why I added that.

Wezi: Sounds tasty.

Me: And yourself?

Me: Already eaten?

Wezi: Yeah

Me: And what are you doing now?

Wezi: Watching the game between Real Madrid and Barcelona.

Me: Which team are you supporting?

Wezi: Real Madrid, even though they are a big embarrassment right now.

Me: Lol sorry.

Wezi: Do you watch football?

Me: I only watch the world cup. ☺

Me: And Zambia. With lots of painkillers on the side. Hahaha

Wezi: Lol nice one.

Me: ☺

Wezi: Anyway, I was just checking up on you. Have a goodnight.

I want to keep chatting with him. About anything and nothing.

Me: Thanks. Goodnight to you too.

"If you keep smiling like that, you're going to have wrinkles around your mouth before you're even thirty," Marjory comments when I put back my phone on the table and stab a piece of sausage from my plate.

I'm grinning like a fool.

In the minutes that I have been texting, she has gone to the kitchen, washed her plate, and come back.

My sausage is even cold.

"It was Wezi *ka?*" she looks at me with the excitement of a child who has seen a packet of corn puffs.

I nod.

"Suited for each other, suited for each other," she sings again.

"I'm starting to dislike that song."

"Get used to it because it will be the entry song on your wedding day."

"I'm not marrying anyone from here. This place is just for work," I pick up my plate and go to the kitchen.

I'm filled with a mixture of fear and excitement that Wezi has finally started talking to me.

As in actual conversations.

Maybe this is what they call butterflies.

I've been in a relationship before, but I don't even remember what I was doing in it.

I memorise Wezi's messages though, the whole thread.

I resist the urge to text Precious about it. I'll give it a couple more days to see where all this is going.

In the meantime, I'll just keep making up scenarios in my head.

Chapter 8

Mweemba grins at me as I take the seat adjacent to his in the boardroom. "You're late."

The room is not big but can accommodate about fifteen people if those are the ones needed for a gathering like this one. The narrow tables covered in Independence Day chitenge are arranged in a U-shape and the visitor chairs that have been collected from various offices are too big for the space between the walls and the tables.

"Oh please, had it not been for the motorbike, I would have gotten here earlier than you," I retort.

I watched him pack the bike outside three minutes ago while I was rushing here.

"How are you?" he says.

"I'm good," I'm panting lightly from the walk. "What's the gist?"

We've been called for a meeting on short notice.

"I have no idea, but from what I hear, the doc is pissed."

"Whatever it is, I hope it has nothing to do with my section. I already have enough on my plate."

We both turn to face the front when Dr. Chisulo steps into the room.

She is indeed pissed.

This anger, it turns out, is thanks to one of the rural health posts staff. He was found drunk on duty by the district commissioner who had carried out an impromptu visit after members of the community complained to him. Now all of us have to bear the consequences of this dent in the reputation of the department.

By the time the meeting ends, I only have to go to my office to pick up my bag and knock off. Mweemba gives me a lift home on the motorbike.

Marjory sees Mweemba dropping me off but says nothing when I enter the house. I follow her to the sitting room.

"Are you ever going to tell me why you hate the guy?" I ask her.

"I have no idea what you are talking about," she shrugs.

I shoot her a quizzical look, but she is determined to avoid the subject.

◆◆◆

My phone chimes as soon I get in bed.

I squeal for no reason when I see the sender.

Wezi: Hey there

I breathe and count to sixty.

That should be enough time to show that I'm not too eager to respond. He needs to know that I have a life.

Me: Hi you.

I successfully resist the urge to add a smiling emoji.

Calm down Sanana, it's just a guy.

Even if his name is Wezi.

Wezi: How was your day?

Me: Exhausting. But I'll live. Lol.

Me: How was yours?

Wezi: So so. Just mundane office stuff. Compiling reports.

Me: Reports are the worst. My quarterly ones are almost due too.

Wezi: What are you doing now?

Me: Just got in bed. You?

Wezi: This early?

Wezi: I'm watching a movie.

Me: No game today?

Wezi: Not my club playing. Just some boring teams. Lol.

Wezi: Do you always sleep around this time?

Me: Not really, just depends on the mood or levels of exhaustion. Hahaha.

Me: I'll probably read a little before falling asleep.

Wezi: Ahh, I see.

Me: What's the movie about?

Wezi: Guns and dead people. ☺

Me: Hahaha

Wezi: Fieldwork tomorrow?

Me: Unfortunately. Lol

Wezi: Let me not keep you up too long then. Have a goodnight and have a safe trip tomorrow.

Me: Thanks. Goodnight to you too.

I close the chat with him and find pending messages from Precious.

20:30

Precious: Babeghel.

20:33

Precious: Babes

20:35

Precious: Iwe where are you? I need to vent!

20:41

Precious: Have a nice life. I've gone to look for new friends.

I chuckle.

Me: Babes, hey.

Me: Sorry, I was talking to Wezi.

Precious: Hmm, going strong?

Me: Rock solid. Lol.

Me: Talk to me.

Precious: Ah I've even stopped being angry.

Precious: It was about that crazy woman at work.

Precious: I ended up talking to Musenge about it and he just said maybe I should try to be a bit more understanding. Do men even know what venting means?

Me: Do men even know anything?

Precious: Exactly! Men are just boring *mwe*.

Precious: He's even calling. I'll call you tomorrow.

Me: Lol ok.

◆◆◆

I contemplate whether I should ignore the second knock as well or not.

Someone must have told whoever is outside that I am in my office even though I had removed the key from the keyhole. I do it whenever I have deadlines to meet.

An important lesson I have learned over time is that attending to every little issue that pops up only gets in the way of other important stuff.

"Come in," I say.

"Madam, how are you?" Mwansa says when she lets herself in. She is one of the messengers in the district commissioner's office that I worked with during the enumeration.

"I'm good, how are you?" I force a smile, dreading whatever her boss wants from me now. The man always has something to complain about concerning my work.

"I'm fine. Don't worry, I haven't been sent," she assures me as if she has read my mind. She hands me an invitation card, "I just brought you this. The wedding is next week Saturday."

"Oh," I get the card and scan it. It is a very simple design; folded manilla paper with bold print and a colour picture of her and a man whose face I am familiar with.

"I know it's short notice but—"

"It's no problem," I smile genuinely this time. "Congratulations." I look at the card again for the name of the guy. "Kafula from the Secondary School?"

"Yes. We've known each other since we were in high school. We have a child together," she adds shyly.

"That is wonderful."

I'm all in for a high school love story that blossoms over the years.

She hesitates, "I was also wondering if you could bake my wedding cake. Nothing extravagant. Just a cake that we can cut... Sorry, I just assumed that with your job, maybe you bake cakes as well."

"Sure, no problem. I haven't baked wedding cakes per se, but I can bake one for you."

"How much will it cost?"

I've never charged anyone for a cake. And Mwansa has that personality that tugs at your heartstrings.

"Uhm, let's do this, you can buy the ingredients then consider my labour as your wedding present."

"Seriously? Thank you so much," she squeals.

"I'll text you the requirements then you can bring them home once you manage to get them. But I need everything at least two days before Saturday."

"I'll do that. My mother is going to Mansa in a few days to buy the remaining things for the event. I will tell her to add whatever you need."

"Great."

"Well, let me not take up more of your time," she rises to her feet.

"I'll text you in a bit."

For the first time since I came, I have a Saturday to look forward to that doesn't involve me sleeping and binge-watching series the whole day. I google some recipes and make adjustments to the ingredients. I go through the list several times before sending it.

◆◆◆

I left my phone in the sitting room when coming to the kitchen to check on the beans that I'm parboiling for tomorrow. The charcoal on the brazier has almost burned out, but I pour more water into the pot just in case.

"You people with boyfriends, come and respond to your messages," Marjory calls to me.

I rush back and pick up the phone.

"He's not my boyfriend," I laugh.

"Yeah, right." She scoffs and gets up, "I've gone to sleep. Wake me up when you both stop tiptoeing around the obvious."

I open my WhatsApp messenger.

Wezi: Hi

Me: Hey you.

Wezi: This a good time to chat, or you're already in bed?

Me: Not yet.

Me: In bed I mean. Lol

Wezi: Lol

Me: Just finished baking some cakes.

Wezi: For whose birthday?

Me: For the wedding tomorrow.

Wezi: Kafula's wedding?

Me: Yeah.

Me: Mwansa asked me to bake the cake for them.

Wezi: Wow! Nice.

Wezi: So, you'll be there?

Me: Yeah.

Wezi: That's great! I'm going too.

I'll be in the same room with him tomorrow!

Me: Oh nice.

Wezi: Do you have transport?

Me: I'm going with Marjory. She's made some arrangements.

The venue isn't so far from our house, but who wants to walk to a wedding when they have an alternative?

Wezi: Cool. I'll see you at the venue then.

Me: Great.

◆◆◆

The wedding reception starts at 15:00. I wake up early to decorate the vanilla cake just in case they come to pick it up earlier than I anticipated. I wash some clothes, set my alarm for 13:00, and go back to sleep.

Marjory's impatient knock on the door snaps me out of my dream about sitting with Wezi at the wedding. Mwansa's aunt has come to pick up the wedding cake. The older woman carries the cake to the car with utmost care. She informs us that they are almost done with decorations at the council hall where the reception is to take place.

Marjory and her colleagues who were part of the groom's wedding committee already have matching chitenge dresses picked out.

I'm still figuring out what to wear when she barges into my room.

"*Iwe*, you're still naked? I've even bathed and dressed up," she snaps.

"I'm not sure what's appropriate," I throw more clothes on the already existing pile on the bed.

"Oh please, people are looking like drag queens out there and you're fussing over a simple choice from all these nice clothes?" she rolls her eyes.

"I only have clothes for wearing in the field."

"Move," she pushes me aside with her hip and shuffles through the heap on the bed. "We both know it's Wezi you want to impress."

"I just want to look presentable to people," I lie.

"Aha, perfect!" She tosses me the red bodycon dress I bought from Pep stores the time we were in Mansa.

I put it on and pull out my transparent heels from under the bed.

"Not bad," I giggle. "I should have braided my hair last weekend."

"You already have nice hair, just do those *tuma* curly things in front. They look nice. But hurry up."

I rush to the bathroom to wet my hair and apply a curl activator. I tie it into a high puff with curly bangs.

A workmate of hers comes to pick us up in his car and drops us at the venue then proceeds to pick another group.

I sit next to Marjory on the groom's side because I don't see any familiar faces on the other side of the hall. No one will hold it against me. I'm not that significant in these arrangements.

My eyes meet Wezi's. He is sitting on my right in the row in front of ours. He smiles and I give him a small wave.

It's a little exciting that he doesn't have a plus one.

Maybe she couldn't make it.

Or she was given a separate card?

Whatever, I'm here to have fun.

The bridal party comes in dancing to a Fally Ipupa song followed by the bride and groom who look elegant in their attires.

It is a pleasant function, save for the usual longwinded speeches and cliché order of proceedings.

The biggest advantage of being from the groom's side at weddings is that you are called first when it's finally time to go and get food.

Marjory and I get in the line and grab our plates of food then go back to our seats. When we are both finished, I take our disposable plates to the bin outside.

Wezi is standing a few metres away from the entrance. He looks dashing in khaki chino pants and a sky-blue shirt. I catch myself staring.

"Enjoying yourself?" he flashes me a smile, stepping away from the people coming outside.

"Totally. I haven't attended a wedding in years."

And that was back in Mongu. Not fancier than this.

"This is my second one here this year alone. The first one was in February, I think."

"Looks like it's wedding season," I giggle.

"Yeah. Hey, would you like to come for lunch tomorrow?" he hesitates. "I wanted to ask you last night but thought to do it in person. And there's nowhere I can take you so I thought of cooking something myself. If that's ok with you."

I swallow the scream that involuntarily made its way to my throat. "Sure. No problem."

Why is my heart racing? It's just a meal!

"So, can I pick you up at ten? Eleven?"

"Eleven will be fine," I smile.

I would have been back from Mass by then.

The master of ceremony announces that the new couple is about to go on the dance floor and we go back to our seats.

Chapter 9

"The guy who is not your boyfriend is here to pick you up," Marjory announces from my bedroom doorway.

He is right on time.

I change from the dress I wore to church into a pair of jeans and a T-shirt. I pull out my crocks from under the bed and spray my body mist to make sure I still smell fresh.

"Why are you even changing? You looked nice!" she frowns.

"Because it's just lunch."

"What difference does it make?"

"I'll be back in a bit," I say. This conversation won't end if I don't walk away from her.

"Or later," she grins.

Wezi and I stroll to his house. It's about ten minutes from mine. He opens the front door and welcomes me inside. I haven't been inside any of the houses in the complex.

"You don't have to do that," he says when he sees me sliding off my Crocs. "The floor is cold."

And it is. Even with my socks on.

I slide them back on and step inside.

He offers me a seat on the sofa directly facing the T.V and goes into the kitchen.

"Cranberry or orange juice?" he calls from the other room.

I've never tasted cranberry juice so I go for the safer option.

He comes with a carton of Ceres juice and a glass with ice cubes. He places it on the small table, pushing it towards me.

"Thanks," I say.

He scratches his head and points to the kitchen, "I'll just finish up with the cooking. You can watch whatever you're comfortable with."

I pick up the remote and change from the music channel to Lifetime TV.

The house is filled with an aroma of a blend of spices.

After ten minutes, he comes back with two plates of Spaghetti and mince balls. He hands me a plate and settles into his seat with his food.

"It may not be up to your nutrition cooking expertise, but I hope you like it."

"This is nice," I exclaim. The mince balls are filled with the perfect amounts of spices and taste better than I'm used to. "What did you add to the mince?"

"An egg when mixing with the spices and just a little flour when making the balls. My dad taught me. He said he learned it from one of his travels."

"Interesting. Now I will have to start cooking mince like this."

"What are you watching?" he gestures to the TV.

"Hoarders."

"Are you one?"

I laugh, "I can't say, I don't even have space for the stuff that I need."

"Then there's me who's forced to fill up empty spaces."

I look around. His small sitting room is quite spacious because there are only two sofas, a coffee table, and a large TV mounted on the wall. Two slim speakers stand a metre apart on the tiled floor. The DSTV decoder is on a large plastic storage box directly below the TV.

The walls are a beautiful beige.

"Did you pick the paint colours?"

"Not really, they were already in the plan. I just had to make sure the contractor stuck to the quality."

"And when will they build the next set of houses?"

He chuckles, "These things are more political than logical."

I sigh and lean back in my seat. "So, why civil engineering? Not that it's wrong or anything. Just why that specific one?"

"I had this fascination with designing, building, and reconstructing things. Which kind of always got me in trouble when I was younger. Every time my parents got me a present, I'd dismantle it and try to reassemble the thing with a touch of my design."

"That's crazy," I laugh at him.

"In the end, my mum just started giving me damaged stuff to fix."

"Smart woman."

"And you?"

"I didn't have any presents to damage, that's for sure," I chuckle. "I kind of hadn't figured out what I wanted to become by the time I was in grade twelve. But I was good at social sciences and loved cooking, even with limited ingredients."

"Sometimes things figure themselves out when they are meant for us."

"I guess so. You said you went to Samfya some years ago. Was it for school?"

"It was more of a fun trip with my friends from high school. I was at Lubushi."

"Huh, that far? Aren't there good schools in Ndola?"

"Dad went there so my brother and I kind of just did the same," he shrugs.

"I had never been outside Mongu until I went to college."

"Not even other towns within the province?"

"No," I shake my head.

"Then you have a lot of travelling to do."

I shrug. "I think I'm better with routines. Travelling is exhausting."

"It's only exhausting when you do it all the time. I've been to at least six provinces so far."

"In my case, this is the third one. Unless the ones I've passed through count," I giggle.

He chuckles, "It doesn't work that way. You have to spend some days in a town and even learn some words of the language spoken there."

"So how many languages have you learnt?"

"I know sentences in all the seven major ones. I'm fluent in Bemba. A bit of Lusaka Nyanja, and Tumbuka. Dad took us to Lundazi for a holiday once."

"That must have been nice."

"Yeah. Great memories." He takes our empty plates to the kitchen. "There are movies on the hard drive if you like," he says when he comes back.

"Oh, let's see."

He gets the second remote and switches to the hard drive. He starts scrolling through the long list of folders. "Let me know which one."

There are so many. I have watched some and others are not to my taste.

"Marvel fan?" I ask when he scrolls past the Avengers movies.

"Not like those people who are either for or against. I have DC movies in another folder. I haven't even watched most of these. My friend just puts anything he likes when I go home. Yourself?"

"I'm not even a fan of these franchises. I just like movies for what they are."

"Seen this one?" he is on Outlaw King.

"Loved it."

"I haven't yet. I'm a fan of Braveheart. How about this one?"

"Not yet, Marjory is always talking about it."

"It's been on my waiting list as well."

He presses play on *The Greatest Showman*.

We watch the movie in silence. I stifle my cries throughout. It's better than Marjory describes it.

I ask to use the bathroom when the movie finishes. I need to clear my eyes. Luckily, the concealer under my eye is still intact.

It was silly of me to have fallen for the July late-morning sunshine and not worn anything warm when coming here. I hug myself as I step out of the house. It's only 17:30, but it's already dark. Wezi goes back inside and brings me his bomber jacket to wear. It's a little loose but warm enough, and I love the rich fragrance of his perfume on it.

He walks me back to my house.

"Going in the field tomorrow?" He asks when we are outside the kitchen.

"Thankfully, no. Just office work this week," I start to take off the jacket, but he stops me.

"It's fine. You can bring it when I get back. I'm going to the provincial office tomorrow. I should be back on Friday."

"Oh, ok. I'll keep it safe then," I smile.

"Great."

I have to stop myself from staring at him when he walks away.

Marjory is marking some books on the dining table when I enter the house. She drops her pen and crosses her legs, "Start from the beginning."

I roll my eyes and sit down.

Chapter 10

The shop owner asks if I'm ok with my change being all coins and I tell her it's fine. I've seen the smaller notes she's put aside, but I say nothing. It's only 10: 00. I won't let her ruin my day. I've already had a rough week. One day when I'm not in a good mood, I will bring all my coins to her shop.

I throw the coins in the plastic bag containing the salt sachet and walk out of the place. Across from where I'm standing, Wezi is sitting outside a popular bar with Mr. Katebe and a few other guys. The two of them wave at me. I wave back and get going.

I make sure to cook enough rice for lunch and supper. If I take a nap now there's no guarantee I'll want to stand in front of the stove again. It's too much commitment for one day.

No sooner does my head hit the pillow than my phone chimes.

Wezi: Hey, are you home?

Me: Yeah.

Wezi: Busy?

Me: Not really.

Wezi: Cool, I'm on my way.

In a place where human judgement didn't matter, I would go out in this onesie because it's my life. But not here. Here, I have to change into a tracksuit before I meet him outside. I leave his jacket on the bed. He'll probably walk me back so I'll give it to him then.

"You look nice," he says, giving me a once-over.

"Thanks. I like your jacket." He is wearing sweatpants and an even nicer bomber jacket.

He smiles, "Are you up for a walk?"

I stare briefly at my faux fur boots. "Depends on how far."

"Don't worry, it's within."

I haven't taken leisure walks since I arrived. There isn't much that interests me around. My movements are all purposeful. Either to get something at the market or to see a colleague or when I tag along on Marjory's numerous visits to her friends. Coming back home with dusty legs doesn't give me enough motivation to do it merely for the sake of it.

Today's purpose is Wezi.

We stroll through the cluster of houses where most civil servants live. At the end of the dirt road that runs through the boma begins endless villages. We receive greetings from the locals we walk past. I convince myself they are directed at Wezi.

"How come all these people know you?" I chuckle.

"Me? I keep thinking they are your people."

"I doubt that. I've never come this far."

He laughs, "Do you keep count of how many people come to the hospital? And those who attend your meetings? It's only one of you, but the whole district of them. If I'm known yet I only visit construction sites, imagine you."

That makes a lot of sense.

We make an L-turn and start walking towards the football pitch at the Secondary School. There aren't many people moving around on this side. Someone we both know drives past us and we wave back at him.

"The local tournament is starting tomorrow," he says when we reach the middle of the pitch.

"Mmh, there's even a tournament?"

"Yeah, a number of us put together some resources to sponsor it."

"That's nice. So, there are even prizes and all that?"

"Yes. Well, it's not in thousands or anything grand, but it helps with motivation. Most of the players are either teens or school leavers and even dropouts looking to be scouted."

"Wow, it's a great thing you guys are doing."

He watches me pull the hood of my track top over my head and rub my hands against my upper arms. The sun has already sunk.

"I think we should head back before one of us catches a cold," he grins.

The stroll from the school ground is shorter to my house than the route we took earlier. Marjory is still not back from where she went.

"Thank you for today. I would probably still be sleeping if you hadn't come," I smile shyly, avoiding eye contact. We are facing each other.

"Thank you for agreeing to spend time with me."

Neither of us moves.

"Ah, I almost forgot. I should give you back your jacket."

"I'm going to see Mr. Katebe from here. I might just end up forgetting it somewhere. I'll get it some other time."

"Oh, ok." I'm still not looking above his chest.

"Goodnight," he says.

"Goodnight."

Neither of us moves.

He is standing too close.

He smells just like his jacket. Only fresher. Nicer.

The crook of his index finger gently lifts my chin. I look at him.

His eyes bore into mine.

His lips touch mine. Softly. Gently.

I part my lips.

I taste his tongue.

It's…everything.

His hands come around my waist. Mine go around his neck.

I'm lost in the moment. In us. My stomach does several backflips.

He pulls away slowly and brushes his forehead against mine. Our lips touch briefly.

"Goodnight," he says.

"Goodnight."

He waits for me to get inside the house. I close the door behind me and lean against it. I will cling to everything I've felt today.

◆◆◆

I'm lying on my bed reeling from the altercation I just had with my mother on the phone when I'm startled by the sound of breaking glass in the kitchen. I had not heard anyone get into the house.

"Sorry," comes Marjory's voice.

I get off the bed and rush to the kitchen to check what happened.

"I thought you were still at work?" There's glass scattered on the floor, but she is ok.

"I lied that I have a headache. There's a staff meeting and I got tired of going in circles over the same things. My head of department will update me tomorrow if he feels like it." She gets a broom and dustpan to clean up the mess. "The glass slipped out of my hand. How's your mother's day going?"

"Terrible, and I don't even know if it's the pees or my family that is making me feel like this."

"Ah, family drama is the worst. That's why this year I resolved to cut off everyone who tries to stress me, siblings included."

I chuckle, "You're crazy."

"I'm telling you."

"My mother is from telling me that my father borrowed money which he failed to pay back so now the owner has given him a one-week ultimatum."

"Eh eh."

"She couldn't even explain what exactly he had done with the same money. Marjory, I send these people money for groceries every month. On top of paying school fees for my young sister who is in grade eleven; the one whose twin got pregnant when they were in grade nine. My immediate young brother, Kahilu, will be going to college next year and even that is going to be my responsibility."

"My friend, you can only do so much for people. At the end of the day, we're all just trying to survive and be happy."

I sigh, "It's so frustrating *mwe*."

"Why should other people's problems take away your joy? Right now, my priority is me. And I know they're your parents. But if you show them that you will always bail them out, in the end, you are the one who will go into debt. Have you seen some of these people I work with? Their payslips can make you cry. Real tears so."

My mother is a housewife and my father, a former office orderly at the National Assembly office where he was fired for gross misconduct, is now a peasant farmer.

My father's young brother, uncle Masiliso had taken me in as his dependent when I made it to grade ten. He was a teacher at Mongu Secondary School at the time.

I enjoyed cooking and excelled in the food and nutrition subject throughout high school so he encouraged me to pursue it as a career. He also paid for my college diploma course.

My four siblings, however, were not as fortunate. Kahilu completed secondary school three years ago and he is now a part-time bus conductor because he was left out on the government scholarships. He wants to be a dental therapist. I recently spoke to the dean of students who assured me that his spot will be reserved in the next intake since he already has the acceptance letter.

"By the way, a workmate of mine is taking *chilanga mulilo* to her fiancé this weekend. Want to come?" Marjory says.

"*Ndipo* people are getting married in this town," I chuckle. I could use the distraction. "The guy is from here?"

"Mansa, but he has close relatives here. If you ask me, she can do better. Anyway, it's just to support these things. I don't want anyone saying I'm bitter because no one is marrying me."

"Is she the one I heard got a loan for the upcoming wedding? Unlike you, I only hear about these things in passing," I giggle.

"I'm not saying anything. Just send me money for the chitenge. Someone is coming with the material from Nakonde on Friday."

I take out my phone and transfer the money to her number. "And the shirt?"

"Everyone voted for a plain black top."

That won't be hard. I have several to pick from.

Chapter 11

I tilt my head to look up at Wezi. I'm lying on his chest on the sofa. The match he's been watching has just ended. I tried to get into it but got bored and ended up watching a series on his laptop instead. "Hey, what's with the bad blood between Marjory and Mweemba? She refuses to talk about it, but I know there must have been something there."

He chuckles and shifts a little to make more room for me on the sofa. "Shouldn't we wait until we are an old boring couple to start gossiping about our friends?"

"It's actually gossiping about other people that makes couples stick together. Otherwise, what would they be talking about for fifty years without dying from boredom?"

"There may be some truth in that."

I shrug, "So, what happened?"

"Let's just say, Mweemba's wife moved here."

"What?" I jump up and sit straight. "He was married when they were dating?"

"Yes and no."

I glare at him.

"Well, he went and got married, came back, and continued dating her. Then his wife came," he says.

"Wow!" I finally manage to say when I pick my jaw off the floor. "But you knew he had another girlfriend when they were dating?"

He shrugs.

"Baby?"

"It was none of my business. I don't even know what exactly was between them. You do know that I only started hanging out with Marjory after you came, right?"

"Huh," I clap my hands, still recovering from his earlier statement. "Men can indeed embarrass you. So even you there's probably a *ka* girl waiting for you in Ndola. *Elo* me if I find out that you were just wasting my time, it won't be nice."

He frowns, "I thought we were gossiping about other people and not accusing each other of things we don't know."

"I'm just saying in advance. *Ine* I came here without any ties to anybody and I don't want to look like a fool."

He gives me that look of his that, as I have come to learn, means that he has given up on the conversation.

"You've heard," I mumble and snuggle back against him.

◆◆◆

Mr. Katebe puts the vehicle in four-wheel drive, but it doesn't move an inch.

I'm standing a few metres away in front of the ambulance, taking pictures. I prefer to be outside the vehicle whenever we are crossing streams or mud pools. I am too young to go to heaven because of these terrains.

It's also important that I document the challenges. Sometimes people will be out there giving deadlines yet those of us on the ground can only do as much as nature allows.

The only thing worse than being stuck out here is being stuck out here just the two of us.

"So, madam, will you come and keep the key in the ignition or go behind and push?" Mr. Katebe laughs at me.

I would much rather go and push than embarrass myself inside the vehicle. The closest I've come to learning how to drive this thing is posing for photos in the driver's seat.

We both go behind the car to check how much trouble we're in. The weight of the vehicle has crushed the loose logs of the makeshift bridge underneath it and both back tyres are halfway in the mud.

There are only shrubs nearby.

The nearest school where we are going to pick up the others is over ten kilometres away, and there is no network here.

He can't leave me alone in the car and I can't walk to the next village alone. I don't even know how far the next village is. This leaves us with only one option.

We get back in the car. I pass him a bottle of water and some biscuits from my last box. He reclines his seat backwards. I take off my gumboots and place my feet on the dashboard.

"*Ba* Katebe, this district of yours is exhausting," I sigh.

He chuckles, "Madam you are resilient. I thought you would break that first day we got stuck and you had to endure the mosquito bites."

"Huh, is it even resilience? Sometimes you just think about where you come from and that alone motivates you to put up with anything. The only alternative for me is going back to Mongu to settle for any riff-raff. *Elo* after tasting a salary *ine* to go and suffer? *Teti.*"

"I was telling my firstborn who is at Kasama College that if she wastes this opportunity, she will just come back home and start selling in the market like the rest of her friends."

"She's a smart girl that one, I'm sure she'll do just fine." I've met the girl a couple of times.

The second phase of the household survey started two weeks ago and I have been going in the field since.

I mapped out the district into four main routes. We would head in one direction for a full week then back to the boma to take on a different route, starting with the furthest communities.

This was a big lesson I had learnt from the first round of enumeration where I had clustered the points according to wards. The main problem with that method had been that some communities in different wards are closer to each other than those within the same wards. This meant that we had to travel the same routes more than once and spend more fuel and movement time than necessary.

It is also faster for a group of three or more enumerators to tackle one community at a time than having everyone spread out all over the district. If an enumerator's gadget gets faulty, the others quickly chip in.

I remained in the last community to finish up some households while my group proceeded to the next.

The sound of voices coming towards us jolts me out of my nap. I put my feet down and open the door. Mr. Katebe is already outside the car.

A father and son get off their bicycle and come to talk to Mr. Katebe who explains our predicament.

The man tells his son to cycle back to the village and get more help while he remains with us.

I breathe a sigh of relief when thirty minutes later, the boy returns with three youths who are carrying axes and some logs.

They cut the logs and place them under the tyres after pushing the vehicle backwards. Mr. Katebe starts the car while I go to the back and help the team push it forwards. After two attempts, it is out of the mud.

I thank the three young men with a fifty kwacha and we give a lift to the boy. His father says he will find him in the next village where they are headed.

When we reach our destination just before sunset, I take out my phone from my handbag. It's buzzing with 'who called' message notifications. I dial Wezi's number

"Babe," I say before he even speaks from his end.

"Hey, how's it going?"

"Aargh, we were stuck for a while and there was no network."

"Eish, how far are you now?"

"We are somewhere near the junction, just picking up two more enumerators."

"Did you have something to eat?"

"Yeah, I did. I feel hungry though. I'll be shocked if this Nshima does not protest my eating it this past week."

We haven't seen each other for the last six days. He jokes that it's now a distance relationship.

"Ok babe, have a safe trip. You'll let me know when you are near so that I put water for you. I've fried some chips and grilled the sausage because some people don't like fried sausage," he says.

I laugh, "I love you too."

I'm only going to spend the night at home and get back in the field tomorrow morning. I'm working with the same enumerators as last time. It's less stressful with all the supervising while doing my enumeration on top of helping to sort out faulty tablets.

This time is also different because I have Wezi checking up on me every few hours to make sure I'm ok.

It's nice when it's not exhausting. Just because I have allergies doesn't mean I will break.

"Enhe, you've spoken with *ba* babe *ka*? I'm guessing I'll be sleeping in the house alone tonight," Marjory says, walking over to me from the back of the vehicle where she has been packing her bags.

"Hi, you."

"Huh, *iwe*, do we get bitten by the same mosquitos or do they send a special kind for you?" She exclaims, inspecting my arms that have glaring bite marks. "You look like you had scabies."

"At least tell me your experience was better."

"Well," she starts, "I slept in a ward and witnessed a woman who was brought in at night being stitched up. I didn't even want to know how the cut happened. So now I'm traumatised for the rest of my life thank you very much."

"Stop being dramatic," I laugh.

"No, seriously. How do you people who work in hospitals see these things every day and not get haunted?"

"Just like teaching, you get used to it," I shrug.

"Huh, over my dead body."

The other car carrying some of the enumerators drives past us and we get ready to go. A couple of others who had opted to use motorbikes have already left.

Marjory and I are the last ones to be dropped off. Wezi is waiting for us outside the kitchen door, a food warmer in hand. He hands the warmer to Marjory when she gets out of the car. He jumps in and Mr. Katebe offers to drive us to his house.

I attack the sausage and chips before I take a long hot bath.

"I hope he picks me up first tomorrow," I giggle when I join Wezi in bed. "Because everyone will know that I spend nights here."

"So? You don't owe anyone an explanation. Let them choke with the knowledge," he pulls me close to him. "I missed you."

"You know how small this town is. And I don't like being the topic of discussion."

"I don't think it works like that, babe. You can't control what people want to talk about. And they will talk."

Mr. Katebe gives me a knowing smile when he picks me up around 05:00. I'm the first one. We drive to my house to pick up Marjory, who has packed both our bags with fresh bedding and clothes. The others are already outside their homes when we get there.

I brace myself for another week of the intermittent network, bumps, and getting stuck in the middle of nowhere. It is late August, but some parts are swampy and wet throughout the year. The trucks carrying maize from farmers have also damaged most of the wooden bridges.

When my group gets to the final community, we find that the person tasked to communicate that we were coming had not done so. We spend most of the day passing the message that everyone should be in their homes tomorrow and manage to enumerate those living close to the school premises later in the afternoon.

This makes us stay there an extra day. It's within the allocated time frame, but it's always nice not to spend all the nights out here. The goal is to do an effective job in record time and have some mental recovery before readjusting to the office routine.

My entire body hurts by the time I get home. I'm going to be sick on Monday.

◆◆◆

Today's distributions are in health centres within a thirty-kilometre radius of the district. We finish early, but I request to be dropped off at the office to wind up a report that's due tomorrow. I don't want to have to work on it at night because there's no way I'm going to reach home and go straight on the laptop.

When I knock off, I meet up with Marjory on the way and we stroll to the market together.

"I think Mr. Katebe mentioned it when we were in the area," I say.

"You definitely have to see it."

"You said Mutu—"

"Mumbotuta. It's not as big as Mumbuluma and the others. It's more of Rapids than Falls, but beautiful still. We went there on Teacher's Day last year. But I don't think that will be happening this year. Someone got a little too excited and wanted to jump into the river."

I stop in my tracks, "The whole Luapula? Who does that?"

"People are crazy, I tell you."

"Anyway, I was thinking—"

"Rival alert," she nudges me with her elbow.

I don't make sense of her words.

Two ladies are coming out of one of the shops and heading in our direction. When they get closer, one of them greets us while the other one just walks past us without a single glance our way. Marjory returns the greeting and pulls at the back hem of my shirt.

"That's Patricia. The one with dreads," she says. I turn my head to look behind, but she slaps my wrist, "Don't give her attention!"

Patricia with the dreadlocks is wearing a tiny skirt that shows off beautiful legs. She is slender and the same height as me. But she doesn't have a scar on her calf from learning how to ride a bicycle, or a birthmark the size of her thumb pad under her eye that she constantly has to cover up with concealer. Her caramel complexion is spotless.

"She's pretty," I unintentionally say out loud.

Marjory scoffs, "With that bleached skin? Please."

I've heard about Patricia but have not met her in person until now. Not that I looked forward to doing so. She is one of the secretaries at the council. She and Marjory reported for work in the district around the same time and had a brief friendship.

Wezi told me that he and Patricia had gotten together once, but that there was nothing between them by the time he and I started dating. Marjory confirmed this, but she warned me that Patricia had her version of events though.

That explains the hostility. She probably knows that Wezi and I are together by now. I'm not one to fight over a man so if she thinks this is a competition, she's in it alone.

Marjory chats with another customer in the shop while I pick the items we followed. I throw in the Supershake that I'm desperately craving. My menstrual cycle has become irregular ever since moving here but every time the floodgates open, I develop the appetite of a whale.

Chapter 12

Coincidentally, Wezi and Marjory share the same birthday.

Marjory is older than him by a year.

I have baked two medium-sized cakes and cooked twice the amount of food because while they have mutual acquaintances, they each have other friends within their circles.

Two of Marjory's workmates from the school and one from the district office came through in the morning to help with the food preparations.

I also asked Wezi's part-time housemaid to give us a hand.

It's been hours of baking and cooking and marinating.

We usually make a big deal of birthdays. They are among the few times that friends who share the dread of being away from their families get together to have a good time. It helps to momentarily forget the woes of living in a remote district where even basic electricity is a luxury.

Speaking of electricity, it is a miracle that we have not had a power cut today, at least up to this point anyway. The officer from Zesco joked that it is his birthday present to Wezi.

Wezi is at his place slaughtering a goat with his buddies and getting the braai-stand ready. I haven't seen him all morning.

Our house has a very small yard and lots of neighbors around. We opted to take the party over to Wezi's.

Thankfully, his house is at the far end of the complex which allows for bigger space and more privacy. I had never understood why he chose that particular house when he had the option to pick any. Today, however, I'm glad he did.

It is almost 15:00 and we are wrapping up the preparations. Mr. Katebe, who is on hand with the logistics, brings the goat meat for marinating. Luckily, the person we had requested to get us some cabbage and carrots on his way from Mansa has also arrived.

I managed to get most of the dry ingredients and disposable cutlery from Shoprite when I travelled out of the district last week.

I put the jar of mayonnaise in the freezer so that it is cold enough by the time we finish grating the cabbages and carrots. The potatoes are already cooked and cooling.

The vibration from my phone startles me. I pull it from under the pile of plastic plates on the kitchen unit. I have no idea how it got there.

"Hey babe, all done here, anything else I can help with?" Wezi says on the other side of the line.

"Everything is ok. We should be there in an hour."

"All right. I hope this doesn't stress you."

I chuckle, "At this point, I'm always stressed. It's even normal."

"And I'm always here for the massages."

"Ok, my love, let me just finish up here."

I end the call and take my phone to my bedroom before it ends up in the oven.

Marjory, who has kept insisting that she helps out with the preparations, gets out of her bedroom. She aids her friend to carry some of the things to Mr. Katebe's car for them to be taken to Wezi's place.

When everything is packed, the ladies leave for their homes to get ready for the party. Mr. Katebe will pick all of us up later.

Marjory and I take turns to bath and help each other to put on makeup. I pick the thick strap navy-blue jumpsuit that Precious got me for my last birthday. It hangs around my hips more perfectly now that I have shed off at least five kilos since I started work.

"Let me wear my clothes, tomorrow is never promised," Marjory says as she slips on the sandals in the sitting room. "*Elo* these are nice, they even make my chicken feet look presentable."

Her feet are gorgeous.

I gifted her the pink sundress and sandals this morning.

I scoff, "When have you ever been patient for anything?"

"I love, love your jumpsuit. You should wear it every day. Wezi, won't keep his eyes off you," she grins.

"Oh, shut up."

"Now sit so that I fix your braids."

I sit straight on the dining chair, giving her my back.

"I don't even know why you bother with braids. If I had your hair, I would show it off all the time." she pulls my braids together and knots them so that she makes a fancy puff above my head.

"It's exhausting to think of hair every morning. And stop pulling my scalp like that. It's skin, not the bark of a tree."

She pulls one braid on purpose and giggles when I wince.

The party starts at 16:30.

We have invited a total of twenty people, a third of whom have already arrived at this point.

The Zanis officer is the DJ. His playlist is a mix of all sounds across the globe but plays Chef 187 after every two songs. Both Marjory and Wezi are die-hard fans of Chef's music.

I'm not sure if it is because both of them hail from the Copperbelt or the guy is just good. I am not really into rap music.

Playing host is both fun and challenging. I go in the house to get some salt and a packet of ice to add to the punch. Everything is set and going as planned so far. The meats are on the braai stand and the rest of the food and drinks are on a large, old wooden table covered with one of my chitenges.

I'm certain we have more than enough punch.

The few crates of Mosi and Castle for a little later are in the freezer.

My six-pack of Flying fish is safely tucked away. If anyone else wants expensive alcohol they'll buy their own.

When I finish rearranging the table for the hundredth time, Wezi pulls me to the side and buries his face in the crook of my neck, inhaling my floral scent. His beard is ticklish against my skin. I giggle as I gently pull away.

"I love you for this," he whispers.

"You're welcome. And people are staring," I tug at the hem of his Real Madrid jersey.

He pulls me closer and brushes his lips against mine, "As they should."

"Well, they are your guests so you have to go there and talk to them."

"I already can't wait for them to leave," he steps away and winks. "You look hot."

I shake my head and return to my task.

Marjory and I have just finished serving the first round of drinks when a taxi that belongs to one of the local businessmen comes to a halt in front of the yard's entrance. Out steps none other than Patricia, with a cake in her hands.

What in the mother of audacity?

I turn to face Wezi who is frozen in his seat.

Marjory is frowning at me.

People are turning their heads to look at me as Patricia struts towards where Wezi is sitting with a few of the guys. I don't want to be dramatic, but this girl is trying me. She is wearing ripped shorts and an off-shoulder top. It's not even that hot today.

I sigh and count up to ten like those who see therapists do in the movies. I'm not going to let this affect me. Her trashy looks don't intimidate me.

She greets all the guys and Wezi acts cool. For a moment, she is just standing there. I hope she feels as pathetic as she looks.

This idiot hardly ever looks in my direction when our paths cross yet she wants to be cozy with my man whenever she sees a window of opportunity. I've seen her a couple of times at a popular bar where Wezi hangs out. There aren't many decent bars and everyone frequents the same spots. I prefer to drink from home. It's not my place to dictate where Wezi should drink from, or who meets him there, but I get the feeling she goes wherever he is on purpose.

It is Mweemba who gets up. He offers her his chair, relieves her of her useless cake, and takes the thing into the house. She sits down and flips back her dreadlocks unnecessarily.

This is the precise moment that I develop a deep loathing for dreadlocks. Now I have to bury my plans of locking my hair, which I have wanted to do from the minute I got here.

I'm going to burn my Bob Marley T-shirt. I also hate the Lucky Dube song that has just started playing.

Marjory joins me next to the braai stand. Everyone is having pretend conversations as if expecting hell to break loose any minute.

I can pretend too.

For now.

Marjory is holding back laughter when she starts talking. "What the hell just happened?"

This situation is equally funny to me. I'd probably be in a fit of laughter had it been happening to someone else.

"If you have no idea, imagine me," I turn the pieces of meat and sprinkle some water over them. It's an unnecessary task because some of the guys just did that a few minutes ago. But I need something to keep my mind busy.

And my hands.

Patricia leaves her seat, greets some other people then walks over to the ladies that are closest to where we are standing.

Wezi's gaze is fixed on me.

Patricia says hello to us. To Marjory in particular, I figure. Or whoever, since she is looking in our direction but not at either of us.

"Hi, Patricia," Marjory replies with the fakest smile I have ever seen on anyone. "I didn't know you were invited."

"Oh, I had no idea there was a whole party, I just came to drop the cake. I'll be going now."

"Thanks. Well, let me just pack you something that you can eat on your way." Marjory gets one of the plastic plates, puts a sausage and a piece of chicken, one goat kebab, and some vegetable and potato salads. She covers it with cling paper and hands it to Patricia.

Patricia thanks her and struts back to the car.

Marjory turns to me and groans, "I can't believe I just gave that tramp our food."

"I kept waiting for the moment you would spit in it," I giggle. "Look at you being mature. Truly a year older."

She rolls her eyes and goes to pour herself some punch.

Wezi comes over to me. He puts his arm on my shoulder and squeezes me to his side, "Are you okay, babe?"

"Yeah, why wouldn't I be?" I say, looking up to meet his eyes.

"Nothing. Just checking on my woman. Should I bring you another bottle?"

"I'm good for now. I don't want to be a drunk host," I giggle.

"That would be fun."

I shoot him a serious look and he laughs, "You know I love you, right?"

"You said that thirty minutes ago."

"And I'll say it again, I love *you*."

"Baby, I'm fine. And I love you too, now go."

"Let me know if you need me," he smiles and walks back to his mates.

I take out my phone and text Precious.

Me: Guess who crashed the party?

Precious: You lie!

Me: In the flesh, with a *chi* ugly cake.

Precious: Ahahaha. Who in the Jezebel universe does that? Lmao. Your town is full of crazies.

Me: Me I'm just shocked here.

Precious: *Elo* she is lucky I'm not there because maturity is not in my blood.

Me: Anyway, she has left.

Precious: Ok but this is funny lmao. I need that courage in life.

Me: Later babes. This party is far from over and I need to act happy.

Precious: Ok babes.

Precious: Tell Wezi happy birthday for me.

"That went well," Marjory pops up beside me.

"I saw you going inside the house."

"Yes. To throw that fool's cake in the outside toilet." There is no ounce of remorse in her voice. "So, if she put any *follow-follow* charms in it, the whole septic tank can go and camp at her house. You are welcome," she raises her cup to me and takes a swig.

I stare at her wide-eyed.

She is officially my hero.

The party goes on for a couple of hours.

After the last guests have left and we have cleared the plates, I take a shower and slip into one of Wezi's T-shirts. He offers to give me a back rub when I join him in bed.

I let out a soft moan as he massages my shoulders. He is straddling my bare back.

"Babe," he runs a finger along my spine.

"Hmm?"

"Thanks again for the watch. I'm never taking it off."

"It's not waterproof," I laugh.

"I'll wear it even if it's dead."

"That's crazy."

"Done," he says, getting off my back and lying on his side.

"And now, the final present," I wink, getting on top of him so that I'm straddling him. I start tracing kisses down his torso, but he stops me midway and pulls me up.

"Uhm, that one will have to wait till tomorrow. You've been on your feet the whole day. I just want to hold you tonight."

I get off of him and lie on my side, facing him.

"Wow," I chuckle, tracing my fingers across his chest. "Just twenty-six and you're already giving up?"

He grins and pulls me closer so that my head is on his arm, "I haven't even started."

Chapter 13

Musenge or the project officer has been in the district for a few days conducting some monitoring. It's still hard not to blur the lines between him being my superior and him being my best friend's boyfriend, which makes him my friend… Sort of.

We have just come back from visiting some of the project's beneficiary communities. He is now making a presentation in the brief meeting we are having with the district nutrition committee members.

I take out my phone and text Precious.

Me: Babes.

Precious: Whatsup? Done with the field?

Me: Yeah. Your man looks great. What are you feeding him?"

Precious: Special nutrition packs. Lol

Me: Hahaha you're hopeless.

Me: Can I transfer some money to your account then you deposit it into my mobile money?

Me: Got an emergency back home. And there's been no float here for two days.

Precious: You and your village. Send. I'll do it on my way home later.

I send her a heart emoji.

Musenge drops the nutrition posters he brought with him at my office and gives me a lift to my house before proceeding to Mansa.

◆◆◆

Wezi ignores my sulkiness when I to his house. He's already cooked supper. We eat the rice and beef stew in silence.

He takes his empty plate to the kitchen and comes back to flip through the channels. He was watching the news initially. Or maybe he was pretending to.

I get up and drag my feet to the kitchen in the hope that he will say something, but he doesn't. I wash both our plates and the other dishes in the sink.

"I saw your little *ex* on my way from work," I blurt out as soon I take my seat on the sofa adjacent to his.

I have avoided the subject for a record-breaking one hundred and sixty-eight hours. My head feels like it's going to burst.

He glances in my direction briefly and refocuses on the game on TV.

I place my feet on the coffee table and lean back. "She pretended not to have seen me," I continue.

He silently counts his fingers then looks at me quizzically, "Your menses are after next week."

"Why? Because that's the only time I'm allowed to express myself? That's insulting."

"I'm merely making a statement. You are the one being dramatic."

"Dramatic?" It is my turn to glare at him like he is crazy. "So, me trying to communicate makes me dramatic?"

"Sanana, you had a whole week to communicate whatever you want to start. I'm not in the mental state to deal with that now?"

Did he just call me by my name?

"Sanana? So, it's just plain Sanana now," I scoff. "That has just put me in a mental state to deal with a lot of things."

He clicks his tongue and lets out a heavy breath. He presses pause on the remote and turns to face me, "Ok what do you want?"

"I don't want to see Pa—that jezebel near this house!"

"Go and tell her that."

"You tell her, *you* are the one she followed."

"You think I haven't?"

I fold my arms across my chest and look him in the eye.

"If you want, we can go together so that you hear it for yourself," he shrugs. He is not even taking this seriously.

"I will not stoop to that level."

"Then drop the subject. Geez, what is wrong with you today?"

He stands up and grabs his phone.

"What exactly is there between you two?"

"I already told you a thousand times. It was just a one-time thing and I ended it immediately. That was before you even came."

"Maybe she is looking for a *two-time* thing," I press.

"Maybe I don't care what she wants!"

He tosses the remote on the sofa and walks to the front door.

"And where are you going?"

"To get some air."

"Oh, I'm sorry. I didn't know I was taking up all your oxygen."

He shoots me an incredulous stare. I cock my head and look right back at him.

He shakes his head and steps out. The door shuts behind him.

What is wrong with me?

Fifteen minutes later, I text that I have missed him. He leaves me on blue ticks. I call him twice, but he doesn't pick up. On the third call, Mr. Katebe answers and tells me that he will be back soon. After an hour, I hear him locking the doors. When he doesn't come to the bedroom, I get up and go to the sitting room where I find him lying on the sofa. I walk over and squeeze myself next to him, wrapping his arm around me.

He gets up without saying a word and goes to his bedroom. I follow him after a minute. I slide under the duvet and snuggle against him. He moves away and I move towards him. He moves away again and I repeat my actions. When he is inches from falling off the bed, he turns to face me. With my back to him, I rest my head on his arm. He voluntarily brings his other arm around me.

I smile to myself and close my eyes.

◆◆◆

The whole rainy season is not ideal for any type of survey that involves moving around the district, but December tops the list.

The targeted households have either migrated to their fields to farm or to catch caterpillars in as far as neighbouring districts. Or they are simply out picking mushrooms until midday. This is when we can start work. The onset of the rains means that we now get stuck more often.

I'm done with the mop-up phase by Christmas Eve and too exhausted to celebrate the day itself. I don't even wake up early enough for mass.

It's my first Christmas ever away from my family. All these years, I could be away for months, but the December holidays were always for going back home.

I don't feel guilty for being away. Just… different.

Wezi invites Marjory and me for lunch at his house and we watch a movie afterwards.

"Are all Hallmark movies written by the same person? Because I'm yet to watch one where the girl realises that her career is more fulfilling than the small-town

Christmas romance." Marjory says. "This whole quitting everything you've ever worked for just for love is not realistic."

"I know, right? Who even does that?" I add. "And it's always the good jobs."

Wezi eyes me but says nothing.

"Exactly! I can't imagine going back to Luanshya for love," Marjory giggles. "As if I'm mad."

"You're even better. Mongu? I can't even think of anyone I ever had a crush on. Maybe if I grew up in Ndola. *Ai* baby?" I nudge Wezi with my elbow.

He chuckles, "I'm not saying anything 'cause this will turn into a court session."

I pinch his cheek playfully, "You're a bit handsome though. Maybe I would have had a crush on you. Then I would quit my job and nag you all day."

Chapter 14

My allowances have helped me buy many of the household items I need. I couldn't entirely depend on Marjory's things because if she had to leave, I'd have nothing to use.

January, however, leaves me financially drained. I took out a huge chunk of my savings which I didn't have much of to start with, to pay tuition and accommodation for Kahilu and get him a laptop. My youngest brother also made it to grade eight and it was just better to put him in boarding school, away from my parents' issues. My sister is in day school, but she has her requirements.

My parents, in their wisdom, had decided to marry off my eighteen-year-old sister to her baby daddy who was also a dependent in his parents' house. The only thing worse than my sister being married off is my sister being married and still asking me to buy things for her and her child.

My little ray of light was that my brother asked me not to send him pocket money for the first month of school or transport money from Mongu. He said he would use the savings he had from his piece works. Kahilu had made it known that once he left, he would never return to our parents' house. I can't even hold that against him. I thought I would miss home when I got here. But now, I've found more peace in my own space. Spending the rest of my life here suddenly doesn't feel as bad as going to my hometown.

Wezi's rash shows up within seventy-two hours of us having sex. There is no doubt that I'm the one who has given it to him. We've spent the whole Valentine's weekend cooped up in his house hiding from the rest of the world. It's the first weekend in a while that we've both gotten a break from all the field work and general work demands of the district.

He ignores it throughout the day, but by evening, it has covered his entire shaft. He can't stop scratching. I'm petrified when I see the extent of the rash. There is no better way of putting it. It is terrible.

I'm not showing any signs of infection yet. That is normal in women, but I'm scared. I give him a piriton pill which he takes together with a painkiller, against my advice. I'm not sure if it is the right combination. At this moment, it's difficult to give any proper medical advice or even remember most of the little things I have basic knowledge of.

He coils up in a foetal position with his arms between his legs and manages to fall asleep at some point. I can't find it in me to close my eyes for more than thirty minutes at a time. I keep checking his temperature with the back of my hand to make sure he doesn't develop a fever.

Early in the morning, Mweemba and Mr. Katebe come to pick us up. I suggest that we go to the clinic near the hospital as I don't want unnecessary stares from my workmates. It's a lie that only the locals spread rumours in small towns.

I have no idea what is going on in Wezi's mind during our drive, but mine is busier than a call centre.

Does he hate me?

Will he leave?

We started dating in July and he is the only person I've been sleeping with in the last six months. We were using condoms in the early months until we both went for STI screening and were safe.

He may be the one with the visible evidence, but the whole situation is giving me anxiety.

Mweemba skips the line and takes us straight to the lab then goes back to sit in the car with Mr. Katebe.

The lab technician, whom I have never really interacted with until this moment, takes our blood and urine samples and runs some tests. He brings the results after fifteen minutes and calls Mweemba to come in then excuses himself.

Mweemba explains that only candidiasis was found in both our samples. I'm familiar with the topic of candidiasis, but I've never had it before. Mweemba elaborates further for the sake of Wezi. He jots down our prescriptions and goes to the pharmacy.

He comes back a while later with both our medications; tablets for both of us and cream for Wezi. He advises us to go back for a retest after a week. He also writes me a sick note. I take a photo of the piece of paper and send it to the Nursing officer.

Mr. Katebe offers to drive us back home.

None of us speaks on our way back. I request that Mr. Katebe drops me off at my place, but to my surprise, Wezi gets out of the car too.

He goes straight to my bedroom and sits on my bed. I pull out a stool from under my dressing table and sit there, directly facing him. I've never been so worried about an infection in my life.

"You can stop pretending now," I say, kneading my hands together.

"Pretending what?" he frowns.

"I'm not dumb. I saw how you reacted from the moment this happened."

"I found my whole… thing covered in a rash, and you are the only person I've been sleeping with. You expected me not to freak out?"

"So, you thought I was cheating?"

He shrugs.

"Huh," I stand and remove the medicine from my handbag, placing it in the drawer of the dressing mirror.

"Babe, we know what the problem is now. Can we just focus on getting rid of this thing so that I can pee without having to avoid looking at myself?"

"I'm sorry," I mumble, my teary eyes darting around the room.

He takes my hands in his, "It's not your fault. This could have happened to anyone."

"Maybe we should go back to using condoms. I don't want to be accused of anything in the future."

He pulls me to his lap and presses his thumb on my birthmark, "Says the person who claims to be allergic to condoms."

"I'm doing it for you."

"I'm not complaining."

◆◆◆

During the women's day celebrations at the council hall, Mrs. Mushili, the district agricultural coordinator, calls me to the side. I've never had any conversation with the woman outside of her office. And even those are a few. She's not as sociable as her husband, whom I have worked with in the field several times.

I'm genuinely surprised that she has approached me. With an inviting smile for that matter.

I quickly compose myself and return the smile. She may be the boss in her department, but out here, today, we are all just women celebrating our being.

She tells me that she loves the muffins I baked for the event and asks if I could go over to her house to show her how to mix the ingredients sometime.

The curse that came with my position in the district is that I am now made to be on the catering committee of any national event.

All I want to do during public holidays is sleep.

It's not, particularly that I hate gatherings. I spend way too much time around various groups of people in my work life. I could use any alone time that I get.

I agree to meet her on Sunday afternoon.

Because she appreciated my efforts.

And because she's not like most of these women whose only bond is what relationship is trending or who was caught doing what. They asked me how Wezi is doing not because they are interested in *how* he is doing. They want to know if there are cracks in our relationship that they can laugh about.

"What was that intrusive hag telling you?" Marjory comes up to me as soon as Mrs. Mushili leaves.

"You need to stop being judgemental," I laugh.

"She's always preaching to everyone as if her marriage is perfect. I've heard stories about her husband."

"She just asked if I could go and show her how to bake muffins."

"And?"

"And I said I will."

"Ah, tell her you've changed your mind. She just wants to meddle in your business. I know her."

"*Iwe*, I can't just turn around and say that."

"It's not a commitment. As if she is paying you."

"I'll be the judge of whether she wants to meddle in my life or not."

"Don't say I never told you." She hands me a bottle of Fanta. "Drink fast so that you can go and get us another round since they've already seen my face."

◆◆◆

There is no internet in the district and I forgot my flash at home. I grudgingly carry my laptop and walk from the hospital to Richard's office.

He is compiling weekly reports from everyone and it's Friday. Plus, I always struggle with the pie charts and need him to go over them in time.

On my way, I see Patricia coming in my direction and as usual, she takes a detour.

I greet the ladies in the reception area and focus on my business.

When I get back to my office, I text Precious.

Me: How are the reports going over there?

Precious: Hectic as usual. Done *uko*?

Me: Just coming from handing in *apa* so.

Precious: Shine. Remaining with some data from the monitoring. And I have a *chi* assignment that's giving me a headache and it's due on Monday.

Me: Lol

Precious: It's not things I tell you.

Me: How's Musenge?

Precious: He's ok. He said he'll be here before 18:00. *Pa* last he will come and type this report. Lol.

Precious: How's Mr. Nyirenda?

Me: He's fine. He's in the field today.

Me: Met that *ka* jezebel on my way to Richard's office. She changed paths. Lol

Precious: Aargh why do you even bother? Wezi loves you.

Me: This district is just too small.

Precious: Tell me about it! Yesterday I pretended to be sick and knocked off early, only to bump into the doctor at the market.

Me. Lmao.

Me: Ok babeghel, finish your report before you accuse me of delaying you.

◆◆◆

I don't go to church in the morning. It rained the whole day yesterday, but the weather today is good enough for washing so I take advantage of it.

Most of my clothes are dry by the time I'm leaving for Mrs. Mushili's house. Marjory simply scowls when I tell her that I'll see her later.

It takes me about seven minutes to get to my destination. Mrs. Mushili opens the door not more than three seconds after I knock.

"Come in Sanana, I saw you from my bedroom window," she says cheerfully.

I step inside and follow her to the sitting room. Her house is one of the biggest and oldest around. It is within the same area as the district commissioner, Dr. Chisulo, and a few other district heads of ministerial departments.

"Please take a seat and feel at home," she points to the sofa directly facing the television. She seems to be alone at home.

"Thank you," I say. "You have a lovely house."

She laughs, "Oh please. *Ifwe,* we are old people now, we have left all the fanciness to you young ones. I hope I'm not troubling you with this, I know you are always busy with your work."

In her home, she is soft and motherly. The opposite of her office persona.

"It's not a bother. Work is a bit slow these days so I have had some good time to rest."

"Anyway, I managed to get the ingredients you told me to. One of my officers was in Mansa a few days ago."

We go to the kitchen and I run her through the recipe.

When the first pan of muffins is in the oven, she clears the table and leads me back to the sitting room. She serves me some *chibwantu.*

I've not had the drink in the longest time

When I look at the picture frame of her family on the wall, she smiles proudly and says, "Those are my boys when they were just babies. How time flies. The eldest is in grade twelve now and the twins just made it to grade ten. They are all at St. Clements."

"That is wonderful." I've never met the oldest, but I've seen the twins at the market a few times.

"Where's your family?"

"In Mongu."

"Wow, they probably don't even know where you are."

"I didn't even know this place existed myself," I laugh. I'm more comfortable in her presence now.

"And which institution were you at?"

"NRDC."

"Ahh, I see they are still producing the best. That's where I did my diploma in agriculture."

"Wow. That's great. It's good to meet a fellow former student."

"But that was a lifetime ago. Before you were even born, I'm sure," she laughs lightly. "My husband and I met when I was around your age. It was my first appointment. I was an extension officer by then. He, on the other hand, seemed content with driving his father's Canter. It was the only means of transport to and from here back in the day.

"You people think this place is in the middle of nowhere now, but back in the late 90s, it was like time travelling back to colonial days. Even the main road was not graded.

"And men, men were scarce. I mean those who had a good head on their shoulders. I knew what I wanted. If I was going to spend the rest of my life here, my consolation would have to be a partner that made it bearable at least. My then-boyfriend from college broke up with me because he had been posted to another province. It was pointless without any proper means of communication.

"Anyway, when I got together with Mr. Mushili, I made one thing very clear to him. That I was not going to hold back on my dreams just because he was happy with his. He had packed his grade twelve certificate, with good points. From my experience, a lot of people here can be smart but lack ambition. My husband was no exception. I intended to further my studies and my career.

"We were still courting when I enrolled for my degree through distance learning. I was two semesters in when one day he came home with his acceptance letter from Malcolm Moffat College of Education. He had applied for a diploma in teaching. Twenty years later, both of us are master's degree holders. That's the DESO you know." She sighs and smiles at me.

I'm too awestruck to utter anything for the next several seconds. "Wow," I manage to say. "That sounds like a great love story."

"It hasn't all been rosy. But that's what makes life what it is."

I sigh and she notices my hesitation.

"You are a smart young woman, Sanana. You remind me quite a lot of my younger self. Determined and very passionate about your work."

I chuckle. The woman is almost twice my age and has three teenage children, but looks much younger than a lot of her agemates. And she is more progressive than some women around my age. After today, I'm holding her in high regard.

"You don't strike me as the type who can't tell when a man just wants to get in her bed. Unlike most of these other young ladies I see around," she says matter-of-factly.

I smile with embarrassment and pour myself another glass of *chibwantu*.

"I hear and see a lot. It's one of the perks of having a nosy secretary. All you youngsters talk about is who slept with whom," she chuckles. "But that boyfriend of yours, he seems all right. Just don't get too invested until you are sure he is what you want. Men can be very tricky."

I wince at her last statement, but she doesn't say anything more concerning that.

She goes into the kitchen to check on the muffins. When they are ready, she takes them out and puts in a second tray.

She comes back and takes her seat.

Just then, a girl wearing a Girls' Brigade uniform walks in. She comes to me and kneels to shake my hand.

"This is Regina," Mrs. Mushili says. "My husband's niece. She's been living with us since her mother died, a long time ago."

The girl should be around the same age as the twins.

While the boys all have a mixture of their parents' features, Regina is a replica of Mr. Mushili.

"Thank you very much for coming over to show me how this is done. My husband will love them," Mrs. Mushili smiles as she walks me out of her yard.

"It's no problem, I'm happy to have been of help."

"I hope I didn't get in the way of your time with your boyfriend."

"He's at the football pitch watching the local clubs."

She calls Regina to pluck some lemons and guavas and packs them in a plastic bag for me. She also adds some cooked maize cobs.

"You should consider capitalising on your skill, you know. You can make this a side hustle or whatever they call it. Don't just sit on your talents. And don't hesitate to come for more fruits if you need any. They are just going to waste. The kids who come to steal them when no one is around keep messing up my yard."

"Thank you so much, I will look into that."

I'm still thinking about my chat with Mrs. Mushili on my way to Wezi's house. In all honesty, it was insightful. I do talk about deep life issues with Precious and I wouldn't

trade her for anyone. Marjory too, but their experience of
life is as much as mine.

I take out some of the fruits and a cob of maize for
Wezi from the plastic and place them on the kitchen
countertop as I wait for him. He never misses the Sunday
games and the team playing today is his favourite.

He walks into the kitchen about five minutes after
my arrival.

"You've finished with your baking?" he hugs me
from behind, kissing the nape of my neck.

"Yeah." I turn around and brush my lips against his.
"You guys won?"

"Ah, these kids are perpetual losers. That's why I
keep telling you to come and watch with me. Maybe you
can bring us some good luck."

"No thanks," I giggle. "Escort me home, I just
brought you some of these guavas and lemons.

"Hmm, you've already turned into besties?" he takes
a bite of the guava in my hand.

"Totally, she even told me that I shouldn't be
spending nights here."

"Then this friendship won't work."

"I'm joking," I chuckle. "She kind of likes you even."

He raises an eyebrow, "Just liking or *liking?* I mean,
I've never been into older women but—"

"Get over yourself."

"Stay and I'll make mince balls for you."

"Nice try. But you know I hate not waking up in my bed on Mondays. I haven't even decided on what to wear for the week."

"I thought you washed in the morning."

"*Ehe,* but washing is not the same as organising *weh.*"

"Fine, let me take a bath so that I just come and sleep when I get back. I'll pass by Mr. Katebe's on my way."

"What do you two even talk about?"

"Stuff that needs to be talked about."

"Like?"

"Stuff," he smirks.

"Aargh. Go bath."

He reaches for my loose braid and coils it around his finger playfully, "Are you sure you don't want to—"

"I'm not joining you," I giggle. "I've already bathed enough for today."

"Ok, give me ten minutes." He kisses my lips and goes to the bathroom.

Chapter 15

Richard and I have been laughing at Mr. Katebe's ironic pieces of advice since we left the last health post on our monitoring schedule for the week.

It's Saturday and I hate fieldwork on weekends, but I needed to get this over and done with. The quarterly reports will be due soon.

"So that's that *ba* Richard, these women only look different from afar. When you bring them home you would think you married the same person twice," Mr. Katebe says.

"So *imwe ba* Katebe you don't want a third wife?" I ask mid-laughter.

"Ah madam, not in this life. You women are difficult. Even the simplest of things have to be complicated. One wants this, the other one wants that. It's too much work"

"*Kaili* you men can't take hints or pay attention to important things. And instead of resolving existing problems which you created, you run off to find another woman and create the same problems for her."

Mr. Katebe laughs, "But that's what makes a man. We are always seeking new adventures. Isn't that right *ba* Richard?"

"It's true, a man needs some conflict in his life," adds Richard who is now looking at his phone with a frown.

"*Yaba*," I shake my head.

"And if both of those women are not even educated or resourceful, it's worse," Mr. Katebe says as we pass the ten-kilometer signpost before the boma.

"Ah, why should educated women fight over a man? They can make their own money."

He chuckles, "Madam, not everyone thinks like you."

"The way I can leave that *ka* marriage the minute I smell another woman."

"But *ninshi* you already have children," he says.

"Oho, some of us will just carry the children and leave," I giggle.

Richard, who has been unusually quiet and keeps staring at his phone, requests that we drop him off at the office. Mr. Katebe then drives me home.

Marjory is lying on the sofa watching TV.

"Welcome back, *ba* celebrity," she grins when she sees me.

I have no idea what she is talking about and I'm too exhausted for her riddles.

"What have I done?" I slump on the other sofa and yawn. I could fall asleep right here.

"Eh, you haven't heard your own news?"

"*Iwe*, be serious."

She picks up her phone and shows me a screenshot that someone sent to her.

"What happened?" My exhaustion turns to confusion.

"I don't know," she shrugs. "I was waiting for you to provide clarity because there are all versions of what transpired."

I scoff and take out my phone to text Wezi.

Me: Where are you?

Wezi: Home.

I throw my bag in my bedroom and rush to his house.

I'm panting when I get there.

"What's this I hear about you picking fights in bars?" I demand immediately I step into the sitting room.

He doesn't turn to face me from where he is lying on the sofa, watching some sports channel.

I'm inspecting his face for any bruises or swelling, but I can't see anything of that sort from where I'm standing.

Even though I'm upset, I'm still worried about what could have happened to him.

"My day was great, thank you. How was work?" he replies casually.

I take a deep breath and remain standing. "Fine. Why were you fighting?"

"There was no fight."

He doesn't need to ask where I got the news from. The best and worst part about our town is that news travels faster than lightning. Especially news about two civil servants fighting over a girl.

"I thought I made it clear to you that I can't be with a violent person."

"Where have you seen me being violent?" he sits up to look at me for the first time since I arrived.

I hate that he is not even acknowledging my anger.

"What were you even doing with Kalumba? You never hang out with him."

Kalumba is the senior agricultural officer. Cocky and full of himself. He thinks his striking looks make him every girl's rite of passage in the district. He has made several advances towards me, even after knowing that Wezi and I had started dating. I wouldn't date him if we were the last two people on Earth.

"He came to the bar where I was drinking, what was I supposed to do?"

"I don't know, leave?"

"It's not his mother's bar," he hisses.

I sigh in frustration. Wezi is outspoken yet not a confrontational person. Maybe that's just what I have allowed myself to believe. I've only been with the guy for eight months. People reveal who they are over time.

"What did he do?"

He shrugs, "It's nothing. There was no fight."

"Then why is the whole town talking about it?"

"Because they talk about anything. There's hot water in the bucket. I was waiting to come and eat with you," he rises from the sofa and goes into the kitchen, leaving me to my thoughts.

I later learn that Wezi and a couple of his friends had been drinking and playing pool at a bar when Kalumba and his team joined them. Kalumba got drunk and started talking smack about me. That Wezi was letting Richard sleep with me in the field while he was busy praising me for being a decent girlfriend. Wezi got upset and pushed him. However, they were separated before anything happened and he came back home.

I'm certain Wezi doesn't believe the nonsense that Kalumba said because he understands the professional relationship that Richard and I share. Nonetheless, it's very easy for such rumours to create rifts among people, especially since Richard is married. I don't know his wife that well and the last thing I want is an unnecessary confrontation.

I want to go and punch Kalumba in the mouth myself.

◆◆◆

The Covid-19 pandemic has started making headlines in the country and its devastating ripple effects are being heavily felt throughout. There are no cases in the province yet, but the hospital has started receiving

protective kits and we have all been requested to remain
vigilant in taking the necessary precautions.

I pick up the phone and call Kahilu after reading that
all schools have been closed until further notice. He tells me
that he won't be going home anytime soon because he has
gotten a 'contract' from some bus operators to sell tickets to
students and organise buses in colleges.

He took this initiative since crowds are not allowed
and many people are afraid of going to Intercity.

I'm worried about his health, but there is no
changing my brother's mind when he gets obsessed with
something. So, I just repeat everything he needs to do to
stay safe and tell him to call me if he feels as little as an itch
on his body.

I say a prayer of thanks that Wezi's trip had been
cancelled in time. His scholarship and study leave to China
for his master's degree had been approved and he was set to
start school in February. Then came the widespread
pandemic and cancellations of international flights.

I have even stopped watching the news because of
the devastating stories of people stranded abroad. I can sit
through movies that have splatter because, at the back of my
mind, I know it's make-believe. But this is real life.

Chapter 16

Wezi planned to take me to Chaminuka for my birthday. Precious, who follows every travel and tours page on Facebook, found a tour agency called Inonge Safaris. It turns out they have a two-day couple's package for the Africa Freedom Day weekend. With the pandemic taking its toll on the tourism industry, the rates are terrific. Musenge is taking his vehicle for service so here we are, all four of us on a road trip to Lusaka.

"I think we should use the Copperbelt route when coming back," Precious says when we reach Kapiri.

"For real, I've never been to the Copperbelt," I add.

"Not even one town?" Musenge glances at me briefly and focuses on the road.

"Nope."

"Wezi you are not representing us well, my man."

"This one doesn't like travelling," Wezi chuckles. He reaches his hand behind his seat and holds mine. He is sitting in the front passenger seat.

"I didn't say all the time," I roll my eyes.

"*Mwandi* you're not missing much. These people only have the black mountain to show for their entire province," Precious quips.

"Says someone from the epicentre of Cholera," Musenge retorts.

"And yet all of you want to move to Lusaka. In fact, Lusaka is *abroad* for people from the Copperbelt," she says

We all burst into laughter.

"Ok *mwandi* baby at least Ndola is clean," she pats his cheek.

Musenge chuckles, "I'm still thinking of a comeback."

"Ndola has everything," Wezi chips in. "Clean air, tranquillity—"

"And a billboard for everyone, I hear," I giggle.

"Don't start," Wezi squeezes my hand.

"Will this whole covid situation affect the funding?" I ask Musenge.

"Maybe in the long term. The money for this whole year was already disbursed. If anything, they might consider increasing the funds because the trickle-down effect of the pandemic will most likely be worse for developing countries and subsequently more devastating in the nutrition aspect. Especially for most of our people who merely wait for handouts instead of being productive."

"Ha, this year has just been bad guys. First it was the floods and now this disease from hell," Precious adds. "Baby remember that day when the bridge collapsed and you had to go and park at Chita and then take a canoe to cross the lake?" She giggles.

"Ok that was terrible," Musenge laughs. "We had to queue up for the canoes."

"You should have asked the doc to send a speed boat," Precious says.

"It didn't even occur to me at the time."

"Elo that same day the district commissioner wanted us to go together in the field. *Njebele* on what lake?" she giggles

"I think the man just likes you, why is he always summoning you?"

"*Awe* he should take his *like* somewhere else. Baby, even the coxswain said that it wasn't safe to move on the lake *elo* he should come with his confusion? Please."

"*Ninshi* these politicians are the same everywhere?" I scoff.

"Imagine!" Precious exclaims. "Even threatening you with *tuma* transfers. Like dude, I don't even want to be here."

"Like that day *ba* Wezi *aba*, the MP was calling him out of nowhere at 04:00. On a Sunday," I giggle.

"Ah for what?" she scowls.

"Who cares? I switched off the phone since he didn't want to do it. Just because the man is in the district we should stop sleeping?" I click my tongue.

"*Ati* he wanted to meet all the heads of department that morning," Wezi says.

"Campaigning at the expense of your rest?" I shake my head.

"You know how these guys behave. Sometimes you just have to take them as they are," Wezi replies, taking the bottle of water from my hand and drinking it.

"Maybe for you men," Precious quips. "Otherwise, why should a man who's not my boyfriend be bothering me on weekends as if it's a hospital emergency? The problem is that these people give themselves too much importance."

Musenge lets out a laugh, "That mouth of yours will get you fired."

◆◆◆

The Rosa bus is parked at Levy mall at 14:00 as communicated by the tour agency in the WhatsApp group. There are six couples already on board, the majority of whom are in our age range. We get to our seats and wait a few more minutes for the last couple that is on their way.

The Great East Road traffic makes it a two-hour drive to the lodge. I'm too exhausted to even pay attention to its beauty at this point.

At the reception, we are all directed to our rooms. However, we are required to reconvene in thirty minutes for the boat cruise. I would much rather take a nap, but these are paid-for activities. That money has to be put to use.

Wezi and I make a quick change into matching denim shorts and black T-shirts and join the rest of the group on the speed boat. It is surprisingly warm today.

"Doesn't this feel like a downgrade from the Bangweulu?" Musenge whispers to Precious when the speedboat starts moving.

"I didn't want to say anything in case I'm judged," Precious giggles. She turns to me. "And you, when are you coming to visit? You will end up leaving Luapula without seeing the best of it. You only have one life *ka*."

"*Pela* I will come during the four days holiday," I roll my eyes in defeat. I haven't been to Samfya since the first workshop. The last couple of meetings have been in Mansa.

We get back to the lodge after sunset and have a group supper before sitting around a bonfire, playing couple games, and sharing stories of how we met.

It is already midnight by the time Wezi and I separate from everyone.

In the morning I have to drag myself out of bed. We need to go for the game drive early enough to see the animals. My biggest thrill is the Cheetah walk. It has been on my bucket list for as long as I have known that people do Cheetah walks. I do the first distance alone and the second one with Wezi.

Precious, for the daredevil that she claims to be, does not go anywhere close to the animals.

I pass on the cheese tasting, but I'm all for the buffet lunch and wine tasting. I'm a little tipsy by the time I go back to the room for a nap before the next set of activities.

Last on the itinerary are the bush walk and the horse riding. With the light wind in my hair, I get Britt Robertson vibes in *The Longest Ride*. Not even the cold can dampen my mood.

◆◆◆

I rest my head on Wezi's shoulder as the bus drives out of the lodge premises. "Babe, I'm so grateful for all of this," I say. "This has been the best birthday in all my twenty-five years."

"Anything for you, hun. Geez, I can't believe you're that old," he chuckles.

I punch his thigh.

Before we leave Lusaka, Precious and Musenge go to visit her older sister. The two of us get a taxi to my brother's boarding house so that I introduce him and Wezi to each other.

We pick Kahilu and go for lunch at EastPark Mall. Most of the eating places are only offering takeaway service but we find some isolated benches in one of the back aisles.

My brother takes an immediate liking to Wezi. The two go on and on about whatever people find interesting about football. I use this opportunity to go and check out some clothes in the shops at the mall. It's my birthday after all. I pick out some jeans and sweaters and also a couple of stuff for Wezi.

"He looks serious about you," Kahilu says when we have a moment alone.

His smile mirrors mine. People often mistake us for being the twins in the family.

"Why, because he also supports Real Madrid?"

"That and because he is also a good guy. I wonder what he saw in you though," he smirks.

"You're foolish," I laugh. "And you, you look clean. You've even stopped looking like a stick."

"What are you saying? I've always been the best-looking one in this family."

"Oh please, you're just lucky you're a man. Otherwise, there would have been no hope for you."

He laughs, "Ok that's deep."

"How's online school going?"

"It's all right," he shrugs. "Just that lecturers now want to teach even at night and random times in the name of network issues during the designated hours."

"But you're a student. Aren't you supposed to be in learning mode all the time?" I grin.

"*Iwe*, I have other things to do."

"Like what, chasing after Lusaka girls? They will just finish you."

"What can I even offer a girl?" he chuckles.

"That is the most sensible thing I've ever heard you say."

"Anyway, there's this friend of mine who has a car. I do Ulendo for him and he gives me a cut."

I almost shed a tear at the fact that my brother has been taking responsibility for his life for the longest time. He takes nothing for granted and uses any opportunity at his disposal.

I'm so proud of the man is becoming, but I can't tell him that. For no reason other than that he is my brother.

"So, why didn't you just do business studies?"

"Because I can do that without spending money," he smirks.

I roll my eyes. "Have you spoken to your parents?"

"Not this week. I don't have money. You?"

"I wanted a drama-free birthday," I sigh. "Wait, they ask you for money?"

He shrugs.

"Why would they do that? To you? I send them money all the time."

"You have a lot to learn about your parents. You've been away for too long. I talk to Eta all the time though. Yesterday she told me that Mbuyoti is pregnant again."

"I spoke to Eta in the morning and she never said anything."

"You just said you wanted a drama-free birthday."

I sigh, "Your sister loves suffering."

"See why I don't want to go back to that place? I would beat the foolishness out of her excuse of a husband. And mom and Dad escorted her into her problems because for them it was one less person to take care of. Who does that to their child?" he clenches his jaw.

My brother has always been guarded. I had no idea that he has been harbouring all these things.

"What can we do? They are our parents," I say.

In my absence, Kahilu played the role of deputy parent. From my own experience, there's only so much one can do for their siblings when they are equally just a child.

We bid Kahilu goodbye and meet up with Precious and Musenge. We spend the night in Serenje and continue the journey in the morning.

Musenge drops Wezi and me at Milenge junction. Mr. Katebe will pick us up on his way from Musaila where he has gone to buy some fuel.

Chapter 17

I'm leaning against the door frame of Marjory's bedroom. She's still wrapped in her blanket and doesn't bother to look at me. "*Ba* non-essential worker, I'll see you later," I say.

"Ok *ba* essential employee," comes her groggy voice. "Just lock the main door on your way out because the way I feel right now, I don't think I can hear even a bomb. This place is a fridge."

"I never thought I would say this, but right now, I wish I were you."

"I've always been your role model."

"Oh please." I close her bedroom door and leave for work.

I'm wearing a jersey and a coat over the turtleneck. It doesn't matter though, I'm still shivering. And I have nutrition packs to deliver in health centres today.

I hate June.

Every morning I ask myself if I need this job.

I should probably see Mrs. Mushili about those lemons before the lurking flu knocks me down. I've been ignoring the itchiness in my throat for a couple of days now.

❖❖❖

With all the covid restrictions on gatherings and travel, almost everyone is spending the Trade Fair holiday within the district.

A number of us got bored and decided to get a little breather from the boma. We secretly came to Mumbotuta Falls to have a braai.

"Ah, you also got one of those?" Richard laughs when Wezi picks up the church fundraising flyer that fell from his pocket when he was taking out his wallet.

"Is there anyone who didn't?" Wezi chuckles.

"I didn't," I say. "Maybe they came to the office when I was in the field."

"You can have mine," Mweemba quips. "I think I have contributed enough to last a lifetime. Fundraisings every month as if it's rent."

"At this point, I'll just be referring to myself as a *donor*," Wezi laughs.

"Ok in this country we get taxed *mwebantu*," I add.

"*Imwe* sure. From PAYE to black tax, tithe, unions, then add fundraising and pastor's baskets and God knows what else they'll come up with next," Marjory sighs.

"There's even that NHIMA thing now," Richard says.

"That's why *ine*, I also give myself 10%. Before I spend on my problems, I treat myself to an expensive bottle," adds Mr. Katebe, who has just joined the group.

The fire is ready and everyone is braaing their packs while having drinks.

"*Elo* here the way they follow up on these same contributions as if you promised. Yesterday I had to pretend I wasn't at home when the ladies came knocking. The music was loud and it was too late to turn it off. They knocked until they gave up. Even God understands when you're broke. *Mwati* it's his self-appointed prefects," Marjory giggles.

"That's it. There's no heaven for you," I laugh.

"Ah, if teaching those unruly kids is not enough to get me a free ride, then there's no hope for anyone," she says.

"It's like the prosperity gospel has infiltrated every church nowadays because the message is always 'give so that you receive more'," Mr. Katebe says seriously. "But I still believe that at the end of the day, God will judge us for our deeds and not what we gave."

"I agree with that," Richard raises his half-empty Mosi bottle. "Besides, at least the church gives a decent send-off, even though they only give you that attention when you can't see it."

Wezi and I step away from the group when we finish eating and take a little stroll to some rocks down the river. The mild rumbling of the water as it swishes over the slippery rocks is so mesmerizing that I'm scared if I stare too long, I may not want to leave.

I turn my back to the Falls and start making goofy poses for Wezi. He takes several pictures of me and then comes to stand next to me so that we take selfies.

"Isn't today our anniversary?" he takes a seat on a flat stone directly facing the Falls and creates space between his legs for me.

"Do you even know when we started dating?" I giggle, threading my fingers through his when he hugs me from behind.

"Ah, wasn't it this same period when I first invited you to my place for lunch?"

"It was just lunch *weh*, is that dating?"

"I specifically said it was a date," he smiles against the nape of my neck.

"Oh please, I didn't even like you that time."

"Right, so you would have gone to anyone's house if they invited you for lunch?"

"Food is food, my friend." I take out my phone and take some selfies of both of us.

"Send me that one," he says when I start swiping through the pictures.

"Ah, I didn't even do my eye properly here. I'll send this other one."

"But it's the one I like, baby."

"It's my phone. You get the ones where I look nice." I lift the phone and take some more pictures. "Hmm, I love this one."

"You just love me," he kisses the back of my ear.

"You wish," I tilt my head back and he kisses my lips.

"Sooo, when are you moving to my church?"

"Huh, the same church that you don't even go to, *ba* Boys Brigade officer?" I lift my hand and play with his beard.

"If I go next week you will follow?"

"Nope."

"But parents are supposed to go to the same church so that it doesn't confuse children."

"They'll just be confused if they want," I giggle. "After all, even junkies have parents who go to the same church."

"I'll convince you soon," he says solemnly and tightens his arms around me.

◆◆◆

I'm rushing back to my office when the hospital guard asks if he can have a word with me.

My day has already been ruined by the district commissioner who had randomly demanded that I give him a comprehensive nutrition report. Some disgruntled non-beneficiaries had gone to complain to his office, again. I told the man that I would be submitting the reports to the doctor who would in turn give him as per protocol, but he was adamant.

"Yes, *ba* Chibesa," I sigh, hoping I have enough composure in my tone.

I never go past greetings with him and now he is asking for a conversation.

"Can we talk from your office, madam?"

"Ok, you can come through."

He follows me until I enter my office and offer him the chair in front of me.

"How can I be of help?"

"Madam," his voice is almost a whisper. "If it's not too much trouble, I was wondering if you could assist me with just one nutrition pack. It's for my granddaughter."

I look at him incredulously. The man is in his mid-thirties.

"*Ba* Chibesa, you have a grandchild?"

He smiles shyly, "Madam you know these children of nowadays won't take advice no matter what you say."

Teenage pregnancy is not new to me. 60% of the project's beneficiaries are teen mothers. Some as young as thirteen.

I look around the room, there are some packs in a box in the corner that I keep for emergencies at the hospital. The next batch will be arriving next week.

"You should come and see me when knocking off. *Elo* I should not see anyone else coming here to ask for the same, otherwise, you will bring back the one I will give you. These things have owners," I say, with all the sternness I can muster.

"Madam, I would never do that," he chuckles. "Thank you very much."

When he comes back a couple of hours later, I give him two nutrition packs.

◆◆◆

Precious and Musenge insist that Wezi and I go with them to Mumbuluma Falls for Musenge's birthday braai during the Agricultural Show long weekend. Several of Musenge's friends from Lusaka and the Copperbelt have travelled to Mansa too. It's practically a waterfall party and we all have a great time.

Wezi and I are going back today even though tomorrow is a holiday. He has some assignments to finish up and submit. His school had decided that he starts his master's online until the Covid situation is contained worldwide.

"This is our second road trip together," I run my fingers through his hair and snuggle up to him on the bus seat. He let me have the window side. I need the air to manage my motion sickness.

"Second?" he turns his head and his chin rests on the crown of my head. "What about the time we met? And that time you came from the first workshop?"

"What? Those don't count. I didn't even know you. That time you were just some *guy* I met. Besides, a ride in an ambulance isn't exactly a *trip*."

"And now?"

"Now you're," I pause for a second. "Some guy I know."

"Huh, we'll see how well you know me when we get home," he chuckles, threading his fingers through mine.

◆◆◆

"Madam online teacher," I giggle as I enter Marjory's room. She's lying on her bed watching something on her laptop. "I'm asking for your hairbrush, mine has bend teeth and not straightening the wig properly."

"Which online teacher? I'm just watching a movie here," she sits up to make room for me. "How can we teach online when most of these kids have never even seen a computer? *Elo* with this network here. They should have just let us rural people continue with classes because, by the time schools open, a lot of these children will be settled in silly marriages."

"Admit it, you miss them."

"No, I don't!" She sighs. "Ok, a bit. They always drive me crazy, yet every time I'm standing in front of the class, I feel a sense of accomplishment, you know. Like I'm making a difference. Even though I know that most of them will still slip through the cracks.

"When I just came, one of my best students fell pregnant in term three. And you know what the stupid parents said? That they had already spent the money for *lobola* and the husband had the right to take her out of class." The anger in her voice is unmissable.

"Eish," I mutter. "And the police? Wasn't that an early marriage?" I'm not sure why I'm even asking this. It didn't work in my family.

"She was nineteen. In any case, I couldn't fight the owners of the child. The girl was already convinced that that was her fate in the end. These days I try not to get attached to any of these children's problems because they are depressing."

"And now you're depressing me. Where's the brush? I need to wear the wig for a Zoom meeting."

"Check in the first drawer. Why do you even bother with wigs? you already have hair that looks like a wig."

"*Iwe*, just focus on your movie."

I take out the brush and walk out of her room.

Chapter 18

Last year was the worst. Covid left the world on its knees. Fieldwork was not affected that much for us in rural towns but a lot of the work meetings that would have normally been held out of the district turned into Zoom meetings.

The paranoia is still lingering in the air. Even after the vaccination. I'm especially worried that Wezi is going to the country where it all started. He was cleared to travel and his semester starts next week.

I've spent the last couple of months trying my best not to think about this day. But the further I shoved the thoughts away, the faster the days moved. Until now, I never thought it was possible to miss someone before they even leave. Above all, I'm proud of him. Wezi is ambitious. Not even the setback from the pandemic had changed his mind about going through with his master's degree.

So here I am, happy on my face while dying inside. This is the longest we are going to be apart. I have no idea what a long-distance relationship is like let alone one with a partner abroad.

Wezi has been doing his best to cheer me up all week. I don't know if he is doing that for me or himself.

This is so hard.

Mweemba is driving us to the junction in his car. He and Wezi are sitting in front, but Wezi keeps looking back at me to hold my hand or ask me to contribute to anything they start talking about.

I don't want to talk.

I don't want him to go.

I'm scared that if I open my mouth for more than thirty seconds, I'll start to cry.

And then I cry.

When he hugs me goodbye.

On the drive home.

He texts me when he arrives in Mansa where he will spend the night and proceed to Ndola tomorrow.

He texts me when he gets on the plane from Ndola to Lusaka and right before he boards the international flight.

And the long wait begins.

The only thing I can't stand more than the distance between Zambia and China is the time difference between the two countries.

I'm asleep when Wezi is awake and when I'm fully awake to talk, he is in class. To top it all, the network here is not strong enough for WeChat calls most of the time. The alternative is voice messaging. I'm not into voice notes because they feel like I'm talking to myself. Pausing and responding to three different points is draining and does not give the same emotional connection as a call does.

Texting is even better since the responses are more immediate. However, Wezi prefers to hear my voice so I make the compromise.

Going in the field means I don't get to use the small period between 06:00 and 08:00 when I usually wake up and get ready for work to talk to him. I can't help but regret not having appreciated the times he would check on me every other hour and I would give the same answer. I know now, to be grateful even for the most mundane things in life.

"Madam, cheer up. He will be back before you know it." Mr. Katebe's voice pierces through my thoughts making me jump in my seat.

I've been staring outside the window blankly for so long that I didn't realise we had arrived at the health post where I'm supposed to be conducting routine monitoring, like a normal person.

God! I must look pathetic.

I clear my throat and force a smile, "Sorry, I'm just not feeling well today," I lie.

Unless missing someone is an illness.

It should be. Especially if it has been a month yet you can't get used to it.

I slide out of my seat and pull out my diary and bottle of water from the backpack.

Some of the committee members come to welcome me cheerfully and I summon the will to reciprocate.

By the time I get back from the last house on my list, I'm so exhausted that I fall asleep as soon as the car starts.

Another day closer to his coming.

I text him as soon as I get inside the house hoping he is still awake. It's half past midnight where he is.

Me: I miss you so much.

He responds after a few minutes.

Wezi: Hey baby. Home safe?

Me: Yeah. Just arrived.

Me: Crazy day.

Wezi: I can imagine. Was watching some football while waiting for you.

Me: Who's winning?

Wezi: Some team I don't even care about. Lol.

Me: Lol

Wezi: I saw something you'd love on my way home today.

Me: What?

He sends a sealed lips emoji.

Me: You should bring it *kanshi*. Lol

Wezi: Hahaha ok.

Wezi: I'll be sleeping now, babe.

Me: Ok my love. Sleep tight.

Wezi: Send me a voice note before you sleep. Love you.

I take my bag to the bedroom and come back to the kitchen. I pour myself a glass of juice after putting the fresh maize cobs I came with on the stove.

"There's *Munkoyo* in the fridge if you want some," Marjory says from the sitting room.

I put down the glass of juice before it reaches my mouth, "That's the first thing you should have said when I walked in!"

I put the juice in the fridge, get a bigger glass and fill it to the brim with the traditional drink from the 2-litre container that will not last a day if I have anything to do with it. I take a sip on my way to the dining table. "No offense, but *Munkoyo* from funerals is the best. It's like people put their whole hearts into it. How was the burial?"

"You don't want to know," she sighs.

She had attended the burial of one of her churchmates. Local funerals are never short of drama and I know this one was not an exception.

"Who was accused of witchcraft this time?" I grin.

"*Ati* the man didn't pay the bride price throughout their marriage. Her family said they would not bury the body until he pays."

I start to laugh but choke on my saliva. "Wait," I say when I recover from coughing. "People do that? In 2021?"

"Now you know," she giggles.

"So, he paid?"

"His relatives had to borrow some of the money. And some of us contributed whatever amounts we could because that body was going to be in the man's house until whenever. And there are small children."

"Huh. People are serious. I need to tell Wezi this story." I carry the half-empty glass of *munkoyo* to my bedroom.

◆◆◆

Mrs. Mushili smiles when she sees me tapping on her office door. "Come in, Sanana,"

She excuses the camp officer that she was talking to and offers me the seat he has just vacated.

I've been to her house twice since the day I helped her bake muffins. We don't run into each other often but we chat whenever we meet.

I can count on one hand how many people I consider friends in this town. Wezi's absence has also exposed how little my interaction is with a lot of people. I'm not complaining and maybe I need to relearn how to be in my own space without constantly feeling lonely.

I'm here to ask for guidance on how we can incorporate our nutritional supplement project into the district's agricultural activities. We want our beneficiaries to be more productive and self-sufficient by venturing into the gardening of high-nutrient vegetables instead of being entirely dependent on the packs.

Mrs. Mushili lets me know that she will get back to me once she discusses with her team what areas work best for our various plants.

"How is Wezi?" she asks once our professional conversation is over.

At least I'm comfortable with talking about personal issues with her. Whatever is discussed will remain between us.

Most people ask the question with gloating undertones so I just give one-word answers and move on.

"He is fine," I smile.

"When is he finishing his program?"

"In December. But he will be coming for holidays in April and August."

"I see," she says thoughtfully. "Distance relationships require a lot of trust and patience, you know. At least there's even a proper means of communication these days. So, you have no excuse for not making an effort to be constantly in touch *ka*?" she smiles.

I chuckle.

"How about you, any plans of going to school?"

I clasp my hands in my lap. If only she knew.

"I will, soon hopefully," I say. My voice can't even hide my uncertainty. It's one thing to want and another to have the means.

"Don't wait too long if you have the chance. These are your most crucial years. It is entirely up to you to let them make or break you. Once the children start coming, it's hell. You end up settling for Cs if you are not careful," she laughs lightly. "You see, men aren't expected to hold back on their dreams. The whole world roots for them. When they see an opportunity, they grab it without thinking twice. But for us, we are always expected to be tied to something, or someone and put that above our aspirations.

"When we get married, our duty is to our husband before anything else. Then when the children come, *they'll* say, 'But what about the children?' So, in one way or another, you sacrifice yourself more for everyone's sake."

I swallow and shift in my seat.

"It's better if you have an understanding partner, but the important thing is not to sell yourself short," she sighs. "Well, let me not take up your time. I will call you and see how we can work together on that issue. I have a meeting with all my camp officers next week."

"Thank you very much, madam," I smile and take my leave.

I'm lost in thought when I run into Kalumba at the market. He stops to greet me with a silly grin plastered on his face. I simply return the greeting without slowing my stride. I'm not about to risk having to explain myself to Wezi over this fool. I'm still not over the nonsense he said about me.

I meet Marjory and her workmate on my way home for lunch. Her friend has her two-year-old child strapped on her back and she is carrying a baby bag in one hand. The three of us walk together until the lady turns onto the path that goes to her house.

"What's with your friend and the baby?" I ask as soon as she is out of sight.

"Oh, that one," Marjory laughs. "Her maid didn't show up today so she had no choice but to come with him to work."

"Huh! Are you serious?" I glare at her.

"This is Milenge, my friend. Nothing surprises me anymore."

"So, she worked with him on her back the whole time?"

"We all kind of took turns to babysit him in the staff room. He is a pretty good boy."

"Wow," is all I can say at this point.

"You think that's bad? Her previous maid took off with half the baby's clothes."

I can't hold my laughter. "What the hell?"

"Maids for you."

"What will she do now?"

"She's called her mother to come. At least she lives in Mkushi. When you have your babies, make sure you have a relative here otherwise you will cry."

"Ha, no child of mine will be born in this town."

"Right," she rolls her eyes.

Chapter 19

We've been having a combined quarterly review meeting in Ndola with Copperbelt province districts implementing the project. The venue, The Urban Hotel has left a lasting impression on my heart. From the friendly staff to the great meals and serene environment.

I scurry back to the table where Precious and I just had breakfast.

"Managed?" Precious asks as soon as I sit down.

"Yes!" I squeal.

"Awesome!"

I've gotten permission from Dr. Chisulo to stay behind and visit 'family' since the Easter weekend starts tomorrow.

Wezi is coming tomorrow and he asked me to wait for him so that we can go back to Milenge together after his cousin's wedding.

I've spoken to his sisters on the phone before but the thought of meeting his whole family in person is giving me the jitters.

Col. Nyirenda is a retired Zambia Air Force pilot and his wife is a retired nurse. Their first daughter is a nurse based in the UK while their older son is a Major in the Air

Force. Wezi's immediate elder sister, who is a lecturer at CBU lives with them right here in Ndola.

His sister had insisted that I visit during the week, but I didn't think it appropriate. I kept bringing up the excuse that my meetings always ended late. I'd rather they *assess* me in the presence of their relative.

I tease Precious about having the makings of a good actress for always putting up a professional front around Musenge whenever other people are around. Both of them are going to Lusaka for the long weekend, yet they have to pretend as if she is just getting a lift from him.

They give me a lift to the Ambassador Hotel where I get a room within my budget. Wezi won't be in Lusaka until later tonight. He will fly to Ndola tomorrow morning.

I use my afternoon to go shopping for what to wear to the wedding. I search for something simple, yet still elegant. I don't want to look pretentious, but also not too basic. I settle for a long midnight blue halter neck chiffon dress and gold stilettos, picking up some matching earrings as well. I just unplaited my hair so a high puff will do. When I have everything needed, I head back to my room to count the hours until Wezi's plane lands.

◆◆◆

Under normal circumstances, I would have stayed in bed until after 10:00. But there is nothing normal about today. I'm all sorts of excited that I even woke up an hour before the alarm I set.

Wezi's childhood friend picks me up and drives me to Simon Mwansa Kapwepwe Airport.

I'm filled with all sorts of emotions when my eyes meet Wezi's.

"Hey," he pulls me in a tight hug. "I thought we said no crying."

"I missed you," I slap away the tears that have now ruined my makeup.

"I missed you too," he brushes his lips against my forehead. "A lot."

He hugs his friend and they drag his bags to the car park. His friend drops us off at the hotel.

Wezi is smiling at me when I open my eyes.

"You slept as if you're the one that was on a twenty-four-hour flight."

"If we count the times you wanted to show me how much you've missed me, I'm pretty sure I've used just about the same energy," I groan.

"Says the person that kept begging for more."

I roll over on top of him and kiss all the parts of his face, "What can I say, it's been three months. Are you sure you didn't find cobwebs there?"

"None that I didn't like," he kisses me back.

I start running my hand down his torso but he stops me mid-way. "You said you're swollen."

I breathe in and squeeze my thighs together for a second, "Right, I forgot."

"You haven't even opened your presents yet."

I jump out of the bed.

"Imagine, I just saw you and forgot the most important things."

He shakes his head.

The bigger suitcase is full of parcels. Most are mine. There are smaller plastics for his parents and siblings. There's also hair for the bride.

I take out my perfumes, lipsticks, and other cosmetics. He got me different lengths of hair.

There's a separate plastic that has a mustard-yellow jumpsuit. He hadn't shown me a photo of it when buying.

I drop everything and try it on.

"Babe," I run my hands over the cotton fabric while staring at my reflection in the mirror.

He gets up and stands behind me, wrapping his arms around my waist.

"Do you like it," he kisses my neck.

Like? I love it.

"This is my favourite present ever!"

I turn around and place my hands on my lower back. It hangs so perfectly.

"You looked so beautiful in the one you wore on my birthday the other year. And when I saw this, I thought it would look good on you too."

"And it's everything. Thank you, my love," I kiss his cheek and start taking the jumpsuit off.

I've changed my mind. I'm wearing this to the wedding.

Wezi's parents live in Itawa. There is a large old design house that has been refurbished in the centre of the big yard and a guest wing on the side near a small swimming pool.

The bride is a cousin on his mother's side. Most of his family members from out of town are staying with his parents for the wedding preparations so the yard is dotted with a lot of people.

I hold his hand and walk behind him.

"Relax babe," he whispers.

"I'm trying!"

Someone calls out his name and a few women come running towards us.

The chubby, light woman, whose features are all over his face, is the first one to throw her arms around him and break into joyful singing.

"*Kasuli wandi nemwine,* my last born is here."

The other women take turns hugging and welcoming Wezi.

"I have brought your daughter-in-law," he says to his mother when the women step aside.

His mother is ululating when she turns to hug me, "My daughter, you are welcome. Please feel free, this is your home."

She holds my hand and dances around as she leads me to the house.

"My son has brought me a daughter-in-law," she announces, to whoever is listening.

I'm met with smiles, greetings, and stares.

His sister is standing outside the kitchen doorway, smiling. She hugs me first then says to Wezi, "Hmm, *namukula*, you're even bringing a woman home, a beautiful one at that. Are you sure she is from Milenge?"

"Don't start," he warns before hugging her.

"It's so nice to meet you, Sanana. You're all he talks about these days."

I smile sheepishly and hand her the plastic bag containing the gifts. Wezi leaves us and goes to meet other family members.

I spend some time with the women. Wezi's mom tells me not to stress with any of the work going on so I end up babysitting and playing with his sister's two kids.

In the morning, I accompany Wezi on the errands he has to run for the couple until the ceremony starts.

The wedding is an exquisite small gathering at Lafina Gardens. The bride and groom who are in their early thirties are childhood friends. They are both medical doctors, as are their groom's men and bride's maids.

♦♦♦

"Third road trip together," Wezi says when we are settled in our seats on the Likili bus going to Mansa. "Am I still just some guy you know?"

"No," I pretend to think for a moment. "Now you're just some guy close to my heart."

He chuckles.

"Like after the walls of the heart, then the rib cage then you," I giggle.

"At least it's before the boob." He threads his fingers through mine and kisses the back of my hand. "Thank you for coming with me to the wedding."

"Thank you for inviting me. I had a great time. It was a really beautiful event."

"Are you sure? It felt like a hospital," he smirks

"Don't be a hater, baby."

"And I think my mother likes you a little too much, I'm scared you will replace me as her *Kasuli*."

"That's because I'm a likable person," I bat my eyes.

"Aha, you wish."

Had we not paid for the room at Central Inn in advance, we would have probably been stranded. All the lodges are still full when we get to Mansa. The room we reserved was just vacated this morning.

♦♦♦

His house is still clean when we get there. Before I left for Ndola, I had called his maid to sweep and tidy up the place. It wasn't really dirty to start with. I went there with her to dust it every two weeks. Sometimes when I missed him so much, I spent afternoons in his bed wearing his shirts.

I have some monitoring to do in the field, but I'm going to make the most of the next three weeks that we are together.

Chapter 20

I drag Marjory's suitcase to one corner of her bedroom and put my hands on my hips. "Are you sure there are no rocks in here?" She's just gotten back from her school holiday in Luanshya.

"You're just lazy." She dives onto her bed and kisses her pillow, "God, I missed my space! And I hope those haters who thought your relationship wouldn't survive choke to death," she giggles. "Too bad I wasn't around to see their faces when you two walked together."

I go to my room and bring her some of the hair that Wezi brought for me.

She runs her hands through the bundle and dangles it. "Seriously, this is mine? I'm telling you, you've done it all. I won't hold anything against you if you don't show up to my funeral."

"And Wezi calls *me* dramatic," I roll my eyes.

"*Elo* I'm keeping this hair until I go where there are proper salons. I don't want anyone ruining it here. I'll just do cornrows when I take out my braids."

She has plaited knotless braids that can last at least two months.

I went to the salon the morning after the wedding. It's been one month now and the Marley twists still look good as new. I'm keeping them until whenever the spirit speaks to me.

"So, any hot dudes *kuma* holiday where you went?" I beam.

"In Luanshya? Everyone I know has dated *everyone I know*. I ran into my ex though."

"The businessman?" I make myself comfortable on her bed.

"He is on wife number two now. Yet he had the audacity to talk about how he is still in love with me."

"Men," I scoff. "I hope he bought you lunch for wasting your time."

"Lunch? *Ninshi* you don't know me? He even gave me the transport money for coming here."

"You are my role model," I laugh.

"I was on the same bus with *ka* Patricia on my way from Mansa. She was expecting me to greet her first so even me I just looked at her and minded my business. That girl thinks she's all that."

"We bumped into her when Wezi was here. She pretended to be on the phone."

"I don't even know why I brought her up, let's talk about more sensible things. So, you went to his parent's house," she wiggles her eyebrows.

"I already told you about it."

"Now I want to hear it in person. *Ati* his mother hugged you? Ha, they are civilised. He doesn't have cousins?"

I sigh and start narrating from the beginning.

◆◆◆

On Saturdays, I can stay awake in his time zone and give a full account of how my week has been. I find a text from him when I get back to the bedroom from taking a bath.

Wezi: Hey beautiful.

Me: Hey you. Ready for the weekly report? Lol.

Wezi: After you hahaha.

I record a voice note.

Me: Nothing you haven't heard from here. Yesterday we gave a lift to a pregnant woman on our way back. At least this one didn't give birth in my presence.

Wezi: Your turn will come and we'll see if you'll run away from yourself.

Me: Baby pregnancy is not your friend.

Wezi: Yours will be special because I'll be the father.

Me: *Iye* I'll just give the *ka* thing back to you.

Wezi: Hahaha.

Me: I was talking to my mother in the morning.

Wezi: How did that go?

Me: Ah I don't even want to talk about it, it's stressful.

Wezi: But why do you let her get in your head?

Me: What do you mean?

Wezi: I don't know, she just kind of manipulates you into doing whatever she wants you to do then you get mad and start stressing.

Me: Who told you she manipulates me, she's not perfect, but she's my mother.

Wezi: Babe, you said your dad is always borrowing money. Where does he take it?

Me: Just because I asked you to help me out that time doesn't mean you can now say whatever you want.

Wezi: This has nothing to do with whatever I do for you.

Wezi: You're my girlfriend, I do stuff because it's what people do when they care about someone.

Me: That doesn't now give you the right to insult me. Not everyone comes from a rich family like you.

Wezi: My family has nothing to do with this.

Me: Then don't talk about mine.

Wezi: All I'm saying is that maybe you should stop letting people walk all over you.

Me: So, being responsible is letting people walk all over me? I'm a firstborn. You have been pampered your whole life and you don't know where I'm coming from.

Wezi: You think if I was pampered, I would have stayed in Milenge all these years? Just because my parents show me love doesn't mean they spoilt me.

Me: Whatever. Bye.

Wezi: Now you're just being childish.

Me: Then go and talk to someone mature *ba* Wezi.

I don't know what's more upsetting between the direction that the conversation just took and the fact that he is not here.

◆◆◆

I walk past the girl with a crying toddler on a bench outside the rural health centre and take the case of drinks and biscuits inside. The agricultural camp officer is winding up our training session with committee members before the afternoon snack break.

When I pass again, the child's screams get louder. I turn to the girl and I'm about to ask her why she is not breastfeeding the baby when I see the child stretching its arms in my direction. I take the cases inside, remove one bottle and one box of biscuits and walk back outside.

Now that the child is out of the worn-out chitenge that he had been covered in, I get a clear glimpse of his full form. Or what's left of him.

I hand the boy a bottle and he downs half the drink in one gulp. He grabs and shoves a whole biscuit in the mouth.

His mother shifts in her seat and for the first time, her bump is exposed to me. She has no idea how many months the pregnancy is. Neither does she know her son's exact age. She explains to me that she came to the clinic to wait for someone. Her husband who has two other wives wants to go and see a witch doctor who has to tattoo the child to rid him of his *sickness*.

The situation is upsetting. I ask the nurse to immediately admit both the girl and the child. The child is placed on therapeutic feeding and the girl's pregnancy is properly assessed.

I return to the training to wrap up the session. My role is mainly facilitating the smooth implementation of the linkage between the agricultural activities and their nutritional impact on project beneficiaries in the long term. The technicalities are being tackled by the officers I have been collaborating with within the last couple of weeks.

◆◆◆

I have a text message showing a transfer of two thousand kwacha into my mobile money account from Wezi when I wake up. There's also a voice note that he sent after midnight.

Wezi: Happy birthday honey. I hope your day is as beautiful as you are.

He is probably in class now, but I text back anyway.

Me: Awww! Thank you, my love.

Ten minutes later, I get a reply.

Wezi: Hey, good morning.

Me: Good afternoon. Lol

Wezi: What will you do to celebrate?

Me: Ah you're not here.

Wezi: Hahaha the day is yours.

Me: I'll just go *kuma* marching and see what happens.

Wezi: Ok baby, I have class in a few minutes. Chat later. And have fun, love you.

Me: Love you too

The area MP is in the district albeit for nothing but a campaign stunt. The Freedom Day commemoration has been highjacked by cadres. I'm merely going there to show my face and sneak away.

I drag myself out of bed, take a quick bath, and look for a pair of jeans and a T-shirt to wear. Marjory is waiting for me outside with her friend when I finish dressing up. I catch up with them and we walk to the district administration block. There is a small shelter where national events are held.

All the seats in the nice shade are reserved for department heads and those deemed VIPs. The rest of us join the members of the community standing under a huge fig tree. The MP is addressing a group of senior citizens sitting on his left.

"How are some of these people even freedom fighters?" Marjory giggles.

"*Imwe* sure. That man in blue doesn't even look like he could walk 1964," I chuckle. "Aren't all real freedom fighters dead by now? It's like as long as you are middle-aged, you can claim the title."

"When it's our turn I'm sure there will even be twerking at these commemorations."

We muffle our laughter and clap the loudest when the district commissioner glances in our direction.

Mission accomplished. I can now go back home in peace and find something to watch.

Marjory and her friend cook lunch when we get back home.

She comes to my bedroom after her friend leaves.

"Here," she says, handing me a gift bag.

I empty its contents on my bed. "Aww, these are beautiful! I rub my fingers over the two pairs of earrings. One pair is gold-shaped stars and the other is a butterfly with tinny rubies in the middle. I get up and put them in my jewellery box on the dressing table.

"You're not wearing them?" she frowns at me.

"I'm not like you."

"Suit yourself." She pushes the three large bars of Cadbury chocolate towards me. "I thought about getting you Ferrero Rocher, but those are boyfriend responsibilities."

I laugh, "I'm surprised you even kept these this whole time."

"You have no idea how many times I had to resist the temptation. Now open we start."

I get two bars and give her back the third one.

Chapter 21

I fell asleep while we were chatting last night and Wezi is still not over it.

Me: Baby, I said I'm sorry. So now I can't even sleep?

Wezi: Me who stays up late to talk to you, I don't have other things to do?

Me: I don't know.

Wezi: Whom are you chatting with these days? Because it's like you're always too busy for me.

Me: *Ninshi* I'm in the field *weh*. Go and complain to the network providers. You're talking as if you don't know this place.

Wezi: You're home now and I had to text you first.

Me: Because I wanted to eat and bath before getting in bed.

Wezi: How long does it take to type a message?

Me: *Iye*, It's been a crazy day. And I don't want to fight with you. I have to be in the field tomorrow.

Wezi: Sometimes you behave as if you're doing me a favour by talking to me.

Me: Baby how was class?

Wezi: Fine. But this isn't about class. You should change.

Me: I've heard.

Wezi: Goodnight.

I toss the phone aside and scream into my pillow. It's hard to be mad at someone who can't even see you.

◆◆◆

Marjory is out of breath as she enters the house. She'd gone to get tomatoes from the market which she had forgotten to buy on her way from work.

"Who's chasing you?" I ask her from the kitchen sink. I'm slicing a chicken breast.

"Is that Wezi I saw at *ba* Mulenga's bar? I was standing a bit far and there were too many people, but I'd recognise Wezi anywhere. How come you never mentioned that he was coming?"

"If you saw him then I'm sure he is the one. I also didn't know so I'm guessing he is here for more important things," I reply without flinching. Mr. Katebe dropped me off an hour ago. I'm not sure if he was aware.

Mweemba has been in Mansa for the last few days. I bet they came together. If Wezi wants to play this game, I will give him a show.

Marjory scoffs and shakes her head, "What's wrong with you two? It's been what, three months? You should be all over each other."

"But we are not." I slice the last bit of the chicken with so much force that I nearly cut my thumb. "I'm not bothered and neither should you be."

I'm not sure if I'm saying that to her or my heart.

She raises both hands in mock surrender, "You're both dramatic and I give up."

There's a knock on the door and she swings it open. Clement, her friend, comes in. He greets me and goes to the sitting room to watch TV. His family and Marjory's are churchmates back in their hometown. He reported for work a little over a month ago.

Clement is a couple of years younger than me and teaches at one of the primary schools within the boma. We treat him like a little brother and invite him for supper now and then as he settles into the district.

"Shit. If I had known Wezi was around, I wouldn't have invited Clement," Marjory whispers when she rejoins me in the kitchen, closing the door to the sitting room.

"Why? It's your house and Clement is like family to you."

"My point exactly! You know how this place is. Wezi might be misled."

I put the pot of rice on the stove and turn to face her, "Since when do you care about the rumour mongers?"

"I don't. I just don't want your boyfriend to get any crazy ideas. He looks simple but quiet people are unpredictable."

I laugh, "Wezi is anything but quiet. He talks just as much as you."

"Excuse me, I'm not talkative," she shifts her weight from one foot to the other. "It's these kids who made me even start talking."

"If you say so." I turn to the stove and continue cooking while she entertains Clement.

We are nearly done eating supper when there's another knock on the door. Marjory looks at me then stands up to go and check. Almost all our visitors come for her.

"Mr. Nyirenda," she announces as if to prepare me mentally. "Come in."

Seconds later, Wezi appears in the sitting room. None of us is using the dining table because Marjory has turned it into her marking area this week.

I pull the plate of food on my lap closer so that I don't have to stand and greet him.

"Hi," he extends a hand to Clement who is sitting on the sofa adjacent to mine. "I'm Wezi."

Clement shakes his hand, "Nice to meet you, Clement."

He has probably heard about Wezi from the whole town by now. He doesn't even act surprised to meet him.

Wezi sits right next to me, planting a kiss on my lips. "Hi, you," he tucks a loose braid behind my ear and pulls me in a side hug."

"Hi," I glance at him briefly and refocus on my plate. He looks great and smells like everything I love.

"*Ninshi* you people don't say that you are coming?"
Marjory emerges from the kitchen.

She takes the seat next to Clement since Wezi has
now taken her spot.

"Too many witches in this town of yours. Sometimes
it's to confuse them with a dose of surprise," he is still
rubbing my shoulder.

I roll my eyes.

"Well, the good news is that we always cook extra
food in case of unexpected visitors. Let me fix you a plate,"
Marjory offers to carry Clement's empty plate on her way to
the kitchen.

I'm still glued to my seat, eating my rice in silence.
Wezi eyes me and takes a strip of chicken from my plate.

"This tastes nice. *Mulamu* is it you who cooked?" he
calls out to Marjory.

"I wish," she plays along, bringing him his plate of
food. "But I have a personal chef."

He takes the plate and thanks her.

She asks him about his trip the way I would ask him
and they get into the conversation. Clement chips in from
time to time. He and Wezi have a smooth interaction.

After about thirty minutes, Wezi gets up and takes
his plate to the kitchen. Marjory frowns at me and I shrug.

Wezi resumes his position on the sofa, takes my
hand, and threads his fingers through mine as he continues
to talk to the two of them.

Clement thanks us for the meal and gets up to leave. Marjory goes to see him out. I've finished eating by the time she comes back. I'm idling with the dishes in the sink to avoid talking to Wezi.

Marjory takes the plate out of my hand and pushes me out of the kitchen.

"*Mulamu*, I think you can just lock up," Wezi calls to her. "Looks like I'm too full to walk back to my house."

I almost laugh out loud. He figured I wasn't going to go with him to his place.

When Marjory says goodnight and closes her bedroom door, Wezi jumps to his feet and pulls me up, leading me to my bedroom.

He twirls me and hugs me tightly.

"You have no idea how much I've missed you," he whispers against my neck.

"So much that you just showed up without saying," I scoff.

"You were not talking to me," he pulls back and takes off his T-shirt.

"You were annoying me," I stifle my gasp at the sight of his upper body. He is more muscular and toned.

"Can I annoy you in person now?" he captures my mouth with his before I can find a response. Tenderly at first.

Then hungry.

Passionate.

His hardness is pressing against my abdomen.

I moan softly and bring my hands to the back of his head. He pulls me closer and I stand on tiptoe.

His hands are all over my back and I want to taste all of him.

He releases my mouth and grins as he starts to pull up my T-shirt which is his. I had planned to avoid him, yet I'm standing here like a fool. No fight, no protest. He tosses the shirt on the floor and pulls down my leggings. Squatting, he helps me step out of them. When he is standing again, he runs his eyes over my body, resting on my breasts.

"I missed you," he whispers. As if he can't believe that I am in front of him. He lifts me and places me on the bed, getting up only to kick off his jeans.

"Wait," I say when he comes back on top of me.

He stops and stares down at me.

"We don't have condoms."

"Since when do we use condoms?" he arches an eyebrow. He removes my underwear and tosses it on the pile of clothes.

"I stopped taking the pill two months ago."

"Why?"

"Because my hormones stabilised."

"I thought you take the pill as a contraceptive."

"I take the pill because my periods become irregular."

"Ok," he says and cups my breasts, bringing his mouth to suck one of my nipples.

"Also, I don't know where that has been," I gently nudge his crotch with my knee.

"This guy?" he looks at himself. "He's been in China."

I let out a breathless whisper when he sucks my other nipple, "Baby I'm serious."

"So am I. And now he is home where he belongs. Unless he's been replaced," he grins.

I roll my eyes.

He positions himself between my thighs, "Can he come home?"

My cycle has been consistent for the last three months and my calculation shows that I'm within my safe days.

I slowly open my legs to give him more room.

The political campaigns have come to a close yet the mood in the district is unpredictable. Lines have been drawn, but the district is a stronghold of the ruling party and the cadres are not hesitating to intimidate anyone who sympathises with opposition parties.

We've had to halt the project's field activities in the past week until further notice as a precautionary measure. Some of our colleagues were caught up in some campaign shenanigans.

On our last field trip which made us get back home at midnight, we were mistaken for those distributing party regalia by a mob.

The civil servants taking part in various polling duties have all been dispatched by the council and electoral commission vehicles. Marjory's team left in the morning.

I'm simply too exhausted from working in the communities to participate in anything that requires me to go back there.

Wezi's polling station is within the boma. He went to set up the place in the afternoon and came back for supper with two of his team members who are teachers from far-flung areas. He is going back to spend the night at the school.

"So *imwe ba* sister you're not going to vote?" he says when he brings the plates to the kitchen. I'm packing his scones for breakfast.

"Ah, baby, voting is for you people who take these things personally. Politicians are all the same. I'm not waking up at 04:00 to vote for more problems. I was already disappointed in 2016. Besides, my polling station is still my former college."

He scoffs, "That whole time people were going for registration what were you doing?"

"I've already said I'm not voting. Just go and declare the winner by the power vested in you *ba* presiding officer."

"But *ninshi* you are the same people who complain that you want change."

"*Ine* I even stopped complaining. Whoever wins will just feed us the same lies. *Apa* I will take advantage of these same days to rest. *Kaili* even patients won't bother to come to the hospital," I giggle.

I walk the trio out of the house and the two guys thank me for the meal. I hand Wezi a big lunch box with the scones and hug him.

"I need my lunch box back," I whisper. "Otherwise, you and your polling assistants will make contributions for a new one."

Chapter 22

Wezi, Kahilu, and I are waiting for Eta outside Intercity bus station. She travelled to Kitwe to drop her application at The Copperbelt University two days ago. I explained to her that she could make the application online, but she was not having it.

The political atmosphere in the country is calm after the announcement of the final results. We are just waiting for the inauguration of the newly elected president. I took advantage of the slow work environment and got some days off to travel to Lusaka with Wezi and see him off at the airport. His flight is at 15:00 so I told my sister to board the first bus from Kitwe.

Eta meets us at the car park near Hungry Lion.

"Hi," she says to Wezi. "Nice to finally meet you in person."

Wezi reciprocates the greeting.

"We are fine too," Kahilu quips.

"Can someone please buy me lunch? 'Cause I'll just die of hunger right here."

"The bus wasn't stopping?" I roll my eyes.

"You're the one who told me to wake up together with the witches so I slept the whole way," she shrugs nonchalantly.

Eta is the sassier and smarter of the twins.

Wezi takes out his ATM card and hands it to me, "I think I'd also like some last big bite two before I leave."

My sister puts her backpack in the back seat and the two of us walk to Hungry Lion.

"He's cute," she giggles.

"So why couldn't you just apply online instead of making all these trips?" I ask her again.

"Because I didn't want to look lost when I finally go there as a student," she shrugs. "Besides, I needed a break from your parents. Do you have any idea how exhausting it is to live in that house? School used to be my escape, but now I'm just stuck there."

There are no queues in the restaurant. Our order is ready within five minutes.

"Is that why you chose CBU instead of just doing the same program at UNZA? Because it doesn't make sense to me," I ask her on our way back to the car.

She opens the car door and takes out her food pack, "Can I at least eat before attending your interviews?"

Wezi strikes up an instant friendship with my sister. They talk endlessly about civil engineering stuff since that's what she is interested in studying.

I like that Wezi is putting effort into getting to know each of my siblings, even Eta who is the least sociable.

When all four of us are done eating, Kahilu drives us to the airport.

"Every time I hear *KK International Airport*, I get this wave of anxiety thinking about what a big, scary place it is with a huge crowd of people going everywhere. But this, this is too slow and ordinary."

This is my first time being here and I'm not impressed.

Wezi laughs, "That's because the airport you imagine is over there," he points to our left. It's not yet commissioned."

That's when I have a glimpse of the modern building next to where we are. "It better live up to the hype because I will protest."

My brother and sister remain in the car while I walk with Wezi to the departure area. He and I sit on a bench as we wait for the queue to move.

I let out a deep breath and bring my shaky hands to my face to hide the tears. "This is so much harder than saying goodbye from home."

He wraps his arm around me and kisses my forehead, "It's hard for me too, babe. At least this is the last semester. Everything will be back to normal by December."

I hug him tightly and stifle a sob as I wave back when he goes to check in.

◆◆◆

It's the first time since I left Mongu that the three of us siblings are hanging out together. My sister and I have booked a room near Kahilu's school so that he can drive us to Intercity tomorrow morning.

We spent the afternoon buying groceries for our parents and showing Eta some places around town. This has been her first trip out of our hometown. We are now having pizza at Manda Hill.

"What's with everyone in this family and running away from home?" I shift my eyes between the two of them.

"You tell us, you're the one who led the way," my brother quips.

"I got a job!"

"And you've never been back since," Eta retorts.

"Do you even know the cost of a return trip from Milenge to Mongu? On top of sending money to you people?"

"No need to get upset. Our brother here chose Covid over coming home for holidays even when he was doing nothing here," Eta sips on her juice.

"You call hustling for my school nothing and yet you're eating the food I just bought," Kahilu furrows his brow.

"Sanana pays for your school," Eta clicks her tongue.

"Wait until you get in school and see if your school fees will be enough for everything you need."

Eta sighs and leans back in her chair, "I don't even blame you people. Just last week, Mom was in a fight with a woman whom she claimed was having an affair with Dad.

The day before I left, Dad was in a brawl at a bar with another man who claimed he had found messages from Dad in his wife's phone. And if it's not about women then it's people he owes money showing up at the house. I can't even walk with my head high in the streets."

"What about that money he asks for fertilizer and business ventures?" I ask.

My sister breaks into a sarcastic laugh, "That's the story they give? And here I thought you were the most loving child for always bailing your parents out."

Kahilu only shrugs when I look at him. We finish our food in silence and get in the car.

We get back to the lodge around 21:00. I take a shower and get in bed, going over the last text that Wezi sent when he was leaving Addis Ababa.

"Thanks for the clothes," Eta beams as she tries on another dress in front of the dressing mirror.

"I can't believe everyone is now taller than me," I chuckle.

"You should see Sombo. That boy will reach the rooftop by the time he is in grade twelve."

"I miss all of you guys." A wave of guilt sweeps over me. It was different when I went to live with uncle Masiliso, or when I was in college.

"But that's just adulthood, right? I believe that at some point, everyone must find their way in life. I don't even want to remain in the country when I'm done with school. It's a good thing Mbuyoti can't fit into these clothes. More for me," she giggles.

"Do you ever talk to her about her life choices? I mean, you guys are probably closer than I am to either of you."

Eta throws the last of the clothes in the sack bag I brought for her and sits at the foot of the bed.

"Just because we are twins doesn't mean we think alike. Maybe if we were identical, I don't know," she shrugs. Then a smile sweeps across her face, "But don't you worry, after her last baby was born, I dragged her to the hospital for injections. I make sure I'm at her doorstep every appointment day. She won't turn into a rabbit on my watch."

"And when you go to school?"

"Hopefully, she'll be smarter by then. She's the older one, I can't be parenting her and her children."

"Also, that rice in the sack doesn't look like it's ten medas. Just saying."

Eta starts to laugh.

"I'm serious," I say.

"Blame the meda they used."

"I know the meda they used," I scoff.

"Well, you are free to go and buy for yourself. I got what I got."

I spend the night going over what my sister said about our parents earlier. Have I been too blind to see all this, or maybe it's true that I let people walk all over me?

It's a long lonely journey back to Milenge and not even Mr. Katebe's jokes when he meets me at the junction can put me in a better mood. I already hate the coming months before I even live them.

Chapter 23

I sit on my bed and cradle my head in my hands. "How did this happen?"

"You tell me, you're the one who works at the hospital," Marjory shrugs.

"Shit," I mutter.

Marjory throws some tissue over the pregnancy test kit that's on the floor. I've looked at it a hundred times, but the two red lines are still there.

I've had a persistent headache and nausea all week and I thought it was just the microgynon heightening my PMS. But the periods didn't start when they were supposed to. It was strange because I'd been taking the pill for a full month. I always start my period on the third day of taking the last line.

That means...

"Shit," I groan and fall backwards on the bed.

"What?" she says.

"That day that Wezi just came?"

"Yes?"

"I had stopped taking the pill because I thought my cycle had normalised... Oh, God."

"I get that. But what's the real issue here, because I hate being confused."

"Wezi is in China!"

"So?"

"How is this not sounding like a trap to you?"

She laughs, but I don't see the humour in it. "Wait, you think Wezi will *think* you trapped him? Be serious."

"We didn't plan for this."

"You had unprotected sex and you both know what happens."

"He... I thought I was on my safe days. I don't want him to think that I did it on purpose."

"I think you're overthinking this. Wezi is not that kind of person."

I sigh.

She picks up my phone and shoves it towards me, "Tell him."

I frown, "It's night in China. He is sleeping."

"There is no sleep for parents."

I pick up the phone and dial his number on WeChat. Wezi answers on the third ring.

"Baby, hey, whatsup?" his voice is groggy.

"Nothing. I just missed you."

Marjory rolls her eyes.

"I miss you too."

"Ok, baby." I cut the call then I send a voice note.

Me: Hi. So, I wanted to tell you that I'm pregnant.

I lock the phone screen and close my eyes.

The phone chimes after thirty seconds. I unlock it to hear his voice note.

Wezi: Wow! Are you sure? As in for real, for real?"

Me: Yeah, found out just now. Remember that time I said I was on my safe days? I don't know what happened.

Wezi: You don't have to explain anything. Man! This is weird and exciting.

Wezi: So that's how many weeks, five?

Me: Almost six. I got back on the pill some days after because you were around.

Wezi: I wish I was there with you right now.

Wezi: Send me a picture of your belly.

Me: Baby *naimwe* it's too soon to show.

Wezi: I still want to see it.

I lie back on the bed, lift my shirt, and take a picture of my belly then send it to him.

Wezi: This is beautiful.

Me: Ok baby, you can go back to sleep.

Wezi: I don't think I will focus on anything after this news. Take care, I love you.

Me: I love you too.

"Did he sound excited?" I turn to Marjory immediately after sending the last voice note.

"If this is how paranoid you're going to be throughout this whole pregnancy then I'm leaving you alone in this house," she rolls her eyes and gets up to leave.

◆◆◆

It has been one unplanned meeting after the other today. The elections came with some new political figures that I have to run through the project activities. I spent the whole afternoon in the new MP's office and only went back to my office to pick up my bag, but I found some clients waiting for me. It took a while to get done and Mweemba gave me a lift on the motorbike.

My phone has countless texts and voice notes from Wezi by the time I get home.

Me: Baby relax, I'm fine, I just got home from the hospital. I had a last-minute emergency.

I take off my formal clothes and slip into a T-shirt and chitenge.

Wezi: Remember what Mum said. You have to take care of yourself.

He sounds like a broken record.

Me: I know my body. I know when to rest.

Wezi: I'm just saying.

Me: So now I shouldn't even be working?

Wezi: That's not what I mean.

Me: Ah baby, I'm tired.

Wezi: Ok baby let's talk about something else.

Me: Thank you! How's school?

Wezi: Just this crazy paper I'm trying to finish. My supervisor is too particular. Why do you women like paying attention to unnecessary details?

Me: Lol because the devil is in the details. You got this.

Wezi: Thanks. Can I see my baby?

Me: I don't think anything has changed in the last eight hours.

Wezi: Baby just one pic.

I get off the bed and stand straight, rolling my shirt up to the band of my bra. I take two pictures of my belly at different angles and send them to him.

Me: There. Happy now?

Wezi: Always. Can't wait to come and feel it.

Me: Later my love. I have to go and feed this baby now. And you need to sleep.

Wezi: Sleep tight when you do. Love you.

I connect the phone to the charger and go to the kitchen to get some food. Marjory has escorted a friend of hers who came to ask for some plain papers.

Wezi has told his whole family about the pregnancy. Now I receive phone calls every other day from his mother, checking up on me, telling me how to take care of myself, and everything in between. His oldest sister has already emailed me three E-books on pregnancy. She has also sent me an assortment of diets. I love them for showing their support. I'm just not sure if Wezi clarified what my profession is.

My mother's reaction was neither here nor there. It's as if I had even delayed getting pregnant in life. Especially since the man responsible is equally a civil servant. My father only demanded to know when Wezi's family would show up to pay *damage*.

Am I ashamed of my parents? No. Do I think they are the best people to represent me in this situation? Again, no.

I called uncle Masiliso to inform him about my situation and asked if he could step in. He told me he wished things had happened the proper way but I'm old enough to make my own decisions and that he will always be available if I need him to assist with anything going forward.

Wezi insisted that we wait until he gets back so we can travel together for the family discussions.

I'm rummaging through the freezer when Marjory walks into the kitchen.

"I know it's October, but are you seriously trying to get into the fridge?" she asks.

I click my tongue, "That sounds like a good idea, but I'm looking for some mushroom that remained." I continue as if I was not disturbed.

"*Iwe*! Mushroom? Today?"

"Yes, I remember there was a *ka* plastic just in the corner."

"Didn't you cook the last pack when Wezi was here? You didn't even like the same mushroom and said you only froze it for him. You always complain that it's too chunky."

"I left some and put it back."

When I have removed everything, I spot a Shoprite plastic bag stuck in the thick ice. I get a bread knife and stab at the ice several times until it breaks. I pull out the plastic to inspect it.

"Yes!" I squeal. "I knew there was some."

I take out the frozen mushroom and place it in a small pot on the stove.

"I already cooked rape and that's only because you are obsessed with vegetables," she says.

"And now I will add the mushroom."

"What next? Will you want to go and smell the latrine at 02:00? Because I've heard that some pregnant women crave that."

"If I do, will you go outside with me?" I grin

"Not on your life!"

I prepare the mushroom and add it to my plate.

It tastes like heaven.

Chapter 24

It's the last day of the workshop we've been attending in Mansa. I was craving some *impwa* so Musenge drove Precious and me for supper at a restaurant in the market.

Precious is watching me devour a large plate of Nshima and an assortment of vegetables. She's only eaten a lump. Musenge has gone to pay the bill.

"Are you staying for the weekend or we are going together tomorrow?" I ask her.

"You want to go back tomorrow?" she frowns.

I shrug, "I'm checking out *weh*."

She and Musenge had offered that I stay with them in Musenge's house, but I didn't want to be third wheeling all the time. Plus, I prefer the comfort of the lodge when I go for workshops. The meetings are stressful enough. I just want a readily available hot bath and curling up in bed as soon as I eat.

"It's not like you have anything to do. Let's just go to Musenge's tomorrow then we can leave together on Sunday. After all, you need to buy groceries. What will you get before the bus leaves? *Ninshi* the pregnancy made you stop thinking ahead?"

"*Teli* the brain shrinks?" I giggle.

"*Awe* yours has started fast. By the time you reach nine months, it would have disappeared." She turns to Musenge when he takes his seat next to her, "I was telling this girl here that she should come with me to your house so that we use the same bus when going."

"That will be great!" Musenge beams. "We can even go to Mumbuluma Falls tomorrow for a mini braai. It's been a while."

"Thanks, I'd really love that." If I am going to be third wheeling, at least I'll be doing it with plenty of food available.

The two of them give me a lift to the lodge.

I shower and when I get in bed, I take a picture of my belly and text Wezi whom I know is very much asleep. I want it to be the first thing he sees when he wakes up.

◆◆◆

Dr. Chisulo had asked me to pick up some hospital materials from the provincial medical office. Mr. Katebe is waiting for me in the Landcruiser when I get off the bus at the junction.

He asks the two guys that have also gotten off the bus to help him load the boxes in the vehicle and we give them a lift.

Marjory is still at church when I get home. I go to my room to take a nap as soon as I have packed all the groceries.

When I wake up around 14:00, I find a voice message from Wezi.

Wezi: Baby I was thinking. What if we just get married?

He sent it thirty minutes ago and he is online.

Me: Lol

He responds a few seconds later.

Wezi: What kind of answer is that?

Me: What kind of proposal is that?

Wezi: A Chinese one. Lol

Wezi: Serious baby. What's the point of waiting?

Me: So it's to get married because I'm pregnant?

Wezi: It was bound to happen at some point so what better time than now? When I come, I mean.

Me: I don't know. Where's this coming from?

Wezi: From me wanting to marry you.

Me: Planning a wedding is a lot of work.

Wezi: Then don't stress, it doesn't have to be complicated.

Wezi: People just get marriage certificates all the time.

Me: Baby the way you know your mother you think she will let you have just any kind of wedding.

Wezi: I'm not getting married for anyone but myself.

Me: I'll be fat in my wedding dress!

Wezi: Lol I don't care how you look with my baby inside you.

Me: Imagine telling our kids that you proposed on the phone. Lol

Wezi: They'll probably be impressed. ☺

Me: You're crazy.

He sends a picture of a closed ring box.

Wezi: First thing I'm doing when I get there.

Me: Can I see it?

Wezi: Where's the fun in that? ☺

Me: Baby?

Wezi: Later love, forgot to get something at the supermarket.

Me: Not fair.

I get up from the bed and scurry out of the room.

"Wezi asked me to marry him," I announce without bothering to knock before entering Marjory's bedroom.

"So why am I not hearing the excitement in your voice?" she sits up to give me all her attention.

"I don't know," I shrug and sit at the foot of her bed.

"Is it the pregnancy hormones again? Because I have to tell you, I can't keep up with your new personalities."

"I just feel like… Wezi is the only guy I've dated since I got here."

"So?" she frowns

"Is it possible that maybe I didn't allow myself to meet different people and maybe know for sure if the relationship is not just because we are both confined in *this* place?"

She sighs, "Is the sex good?"

I glare at her, "Be serious." I've never shared the explicit details of my sex life with my friends.

"I am. Life is too short to be with a man that bores you in bed. Is the sex good?"

"Of course," I roll my eyes.

"And he has a good job. He also comes from a decent and rich family."

I scoff at her last two words.

"Most importantly, he loves you. Do you know how many women would kill to be in your shoes *iwe*? Except me of course. I'm not into light guys. I like them dark and a bit ugly so that I'm the only one who draws attention when we are walking together."

"You need help," I manage a laugh.

"Look, it may be the only relationship, but you got a good one. Unless you also want the likes of Kalumba."

"Yikes."

"My point exactly."

"But, do you think he would have proposed if I wasn't pregnant?"

She sighs in frustration, "Why do you always overanalyse things, Sanana? He wants to marry you. That's what's important. Now if you don't mind, I have lesson plans to make."

I get up and walk to the door. "I'll come back when I have another situation to *overanalyse*."

"No. And congratulations."

I go back to my room and text Precious.

Me: China man proposed.

Precious: Wiyu wiyu wiyu. Chief bride's maid duty calls.

She sends so many emojis that some of them don't even make sense.

Precious: I'll call you in a bit, let me just go pee.

I can't stand the bickering among the women in this meeting right now. This charade of a district catering committee is always mentally draining. We should have concluded the Independence Day budget and menu thirty minutes ago, yet it seems others have no important things to go back to in their offices.

"Madam Sanana, what's your take?" the plump self-appointed chairperson finally asks for my opinion which she doesn't have use for. I'm surprised she even knows my name. She's never said it before.

Everyone turns their faces to me.

"Oh, yeah, I think that's ok." I had zoned out for a minute. I don't know if I'm supporting or opposing. I don't care though. I just want out of this room. These slacks are suffocating me.

The woman narrows her eyes at me and grudgingly writes down something in her huge diary.

I rush to the district administration block toilets as soon as we conclude. On my way out, I bump into the district commissioner's typist who was also in the meeting.

"Your zip is open," she smiles condescendingly.

"Oh," I run my hands over the front of my slacks and pull up my zipper. "Thank you."

"It's normal this time around. When I and my *husband* were expecting our second, I had to pack all my usual clothes by the fourth month."

Great. I will probably hear about my outside wedlock pregnancy in the Zanis report any day from now.

"Thank you," I say again because I don't know how else to respond. I go back to the room to get my bag and head to my office. I've wasted most of my afternoon.

Chapter 25

I wasn't feeling too well after my lunch break.
Dr. Chisulo caught me sleeping in my office and
sent me home to rest.

I got tired of lying on the bed and came to watch TV.
I'm eating my last bar of chocolate when Marjory comes
into the sitting room.

"By the time you give birth, you will be the weight
of a full-grown elephant," she says, walking past me to her
bedroom.

"Back to sender."

She comes back after a while and goes into the
kitchen. "Where on earth did you even find the dried
mushroom?" she calls to me when she checks the pots.

"Trust me, you don't want to know."

Last week, I contacted a committee member from
one of the communities and begged him to turn the entire
district upside down if he had to. He brought a whole meda
to the office earlier today. I paid him twice the initial cost.

"Clement was saying hi," she says.

"Thanks. It's been a while. How is he?"

"He won't tell me, but I'm sure he has a *ka*
girlfriend."

"And you're upset because?"

"He's a good kid. And the breadwinner in his family. If he messes up, his mother will have a heart attack."

"Well, he's old enough to live with the consequences of his mistakes," I stand up, but the sharp piercing in my lower back makes me yelp and cling to the arm of the sofa.

"Eh eh. Are you ok?"

I wince and sit back slowly, "I don't know, I think I stood up too fast."

"What do you want, I get it for you?"

"My phone. It's on the bed. I wanted it to charge without disturbance."

She goes to my bedroom and comes back with the phone. Her face is soaked in worry. "Have you told Wezi how you're feeling?"

"Ah, so that he starts lecturing me? I'm fine."

"This doesn't look like fine to me."

"It's fine to me."

"If you say so." She sighs, "Can I use your laptop to create a template for my lesson plans? That man hasn't finished fixing mine."

"You trust someone from here to fix your laptop?"

"Now where am I supposed to take it.? He managed last time."

"And you wonder why it has a problem again. Anyway, get it from my backpack. Tomorrow you might say your children failed because I didn't lend you a laptop."

When the episode of Mpali finishes, I get up slowly and walk to the bedroom. I change into my night shorts and one of Wezi's T-shirts.

◆◆◆

The piercing jolts me out of my sleep. This time it's in my lower abdomen. Before I can even make sense of what's happening, the warm liquid is between my thighs. Turning to my side, I bring one hand to my groin area.

It's wet.

I'm wet.

I throw off the thin duvet and gently rise from the bed. Everything trickles down to my feet as soon as they touch the floor. I call out Marjory's name a couple of times. There's no response. I take a deep breath and try not to dwell on what's happening.

I inch towards the door and switch on the light, but avoid looking down at my body.

I drag myself across the sitting room and bang on Marjory's door.

She is groggy when she opens it. The look on my face wipes out all the sleep in her eyes.

"Sanana?"

I point at my feet and she follows the trail of my finger.

"Oh, my God!" She steps back and throws her hand over her eyes. "Oh my God, Sanana."

I'm terrified and she is panicking. She rushes past me to the kitchen and comes back into her bedroom. I don't know what to do with myself so I slide to the floor, leaning against the wall.

She is frantically telling Mr. Katebe on the phone to hurry up.

Her whole body is shaking when she picks me up from the floor and helps me sit in a garden chair.

I can't look at myself.

I don't want to.

Marjory scurries around the house, back and forth to my bedroom.

To her bedroom.

To the kitchen.

She starts opening the kitchen door.

Mr. Katebe comes into the house with his first wife. The woman doesn't flinch at the sight of my state. She gently wraps a chitenge around my waist and together they aid me to the ambulance.

Marjory hurriedly locks the house and joins us in the car.

◆◆◆

Dr. Chisulo is keeping me under observation in one of the hospital side rooms.

"Just talk to him, Sanana. I've run out of things to tell him," Marjory pleads as she hands me my ringing phone. "He is worried."

Wezi has been calling since morning.

I would have appreciated the respect of being the one to tell him about what transpired, but this town is full of people who are more interested in being the first to break the news than its effect.

The relentless tears sting my eyes again. I face away from her and stifle a long sob. I loathe everything about my life right now. Someone should tell me what I'm being punished for.

Marjory picks up the call and lies for the millionth time that I'm sleeping.

The only person I've spoken to on the phone is Precious. She said she will jump on the first bus tomorrow.

Later in the day, Mrs. Mushili comes to see me. She relieves Marjory of being at my bedside for the night. She makes me eat the lemon-flavoured porridge that she brought and helps me with my bath.

"Thank you so much for being here," I force a smile after she covers me with a blanket on the bed.

"That's nothing to thank me for. You should know that you have a family even here, among all of us. Also, remember that what you're going through is not your fault and it shall pass. You have to stay strong for yourself."

I have been told that only someone going through pain can understand its depth. So, while I appreciate the sincerity of her words, they do nothing to change how I feel.

I bring my trembling hand to my belly. This has become a reflex action since the day I confirmed the existence of life inside me. All my protective instincts were ignited. Before, doing so gave me a sense of excitement. I had started planning my life around this baby. Every day, I thought of possible names. Perhaps an amalgamation of mine and Wezi's, an exotic place, or something that connotes kingship. I hadn't wanted a scan because I loved the idea of not knowing the gender until the baby was born.

It's pointless to rub the belly now. It's just a reminder of dead hope and what would have been.

I turn to my side and pick up my phone. I open the unread messages.

18:30

Wezi: Baby, please talk to me.

17:00

Wezi: I hope you're ok. I miss you.

16:15

Wezi: Baby talk to me.

15:05

Wezi: I just want to hear your voice.

14:21

Wezi: Baby pick up the phone. Please.

11:05

Wezi: Are you ok? I'm worried.

10: 17

Wezi: Baby what happened?

There are countless calls in between.

Wezi was obsessed with the baby. All our recent conversations had been about the baby. He asked me to marry him because of the baby. I don't know what to say, but I have to tell him something.

Me: Hi, still at the hospital. Been cleaned up. Still feeling some pain.

He calls as soon as my message is delivered. He says he hasn't been able to sleep. There's urgency but mostly worry in his voice. I force myself to speak. My voice is still croaky from the crying and prolonged silence. The bad reception is also making me have to repeat myself now and then. He tells me not to blame myself for what happened and some other stuff that I'm zoning in and out of.

He texts after he ends the call.

Wezi: I wish I was there with you. I miss you a lot.

Me: Me too.

Wezi: Get some rest. I love you.

Me: I love you too.

I don't want to rest. I want to get out of this bed, out of this hospital, and out of this void that's sucking me!

Chapter 26

Marjory comes to see me on her way to work.

"I told my head of department that I'd be a little late today. If not for the test, I wouldn't have even gone," she says. I can only imagine how traumatising this has been for her.

"If not for the money, you wouldn't even be working," my chuckle is weak.

"I think my calling is being a trophy wife." Not even her smile can cover up her dispirited tone. "I'll come as soon as I can."

Mrs. Mushili leaves when Precious arrives.

"Hi you," Precious says, dropping her overnight bag and backpack on the chair that has just been vacated. She sits at the foot of my bed.

"Thanks for coming," I sit up and prop my head on the pillow against the wall. "It means everything."

"Remember that day I showed up late for the test that you wrote half of for me?" she chuckles. "I don't even remember the series that made me sleep late. The plan was to watch only one episode to refresh my mind. I didn't even manage to do more revision in the morning because I didn't hear the alarm. *Elo ka* Jayden also didn't come to my room to make noise. Everything was just working against me *mwe*. The *chi* bus also died at Hybrid."

"The way you were panting when you got in class," I manage a light laugh.

"And then Mr. Haanzala just scowled at me and told me to go and sit down. I was expecting him to send me back."

"I don't even know why you went home that weekend when being late is your talent."

"*Iwe*, there was cake at home that weekend, and my sister's maid has *tuma* manners of not asking if she can carry leftovers. After all, you ate some."

"Obviously, I earned it. You think reducing my thinking to your level is easy?"

Precious showed up almost an hour after the test started and we had been assigned ninety minutes only. I took the initiative to start writing for her and handed her the answer sheet stacked between blank papers. The lecturer added the results of that test to our overall end-of-term results because a lot of students were in the habit of shunning monthly tests.

"That was the highest mark I had ever gotten," she giggles. "Now the way you tried so hard to fake my handwriting. Do I write Y like I have long fingers?"

I'm laughing so hard that I'm scared the bleeding will get worse.

Dr. Chisulo comes to check on me and clears me to go home. Mr. Katebe gives us a lift.

I text Marjory to tell her that I've been discharged.

I try to block out the flashbacks of what happened in my bedroom less than forty-eight hours ago, but they still linger. Marjory burnt the T-shirt and shorts I wore that night and the chitenge she had used to clean up the mess, along with the bedsheets.

Precious makes my bed and helps me lie down. I don't have the appetite for anything, but she cooks and forces me to eat anyway. I am so grateful that she is neither being pitiful nor letting me wallow in self-pity.

I can take sympathy, not pity.

When Marjory gets back from work, the two of them do their best to cheer me up. I wish they can do that in my dreams as well because in the dead of night is when the horrific images haunt me. If only I could take a break from my mind.

I received so many theories from everyone who felt they had something to say about my situation while I lay on the hospital bed. 'At least it's just the first trimester, the second would have been worse'. 'You are lucky that it was just a pregnancy, a fully developed child is more painful to lose'. And the worst of them all, 'it was God's will'.

Why would God will such a horrendous thing?

◆◆◆

Precious is leaving and I can't even escort her up to the junction because of the discomfort.

"This isn't such a bad place after all." She steps into the car that's here to take her to the main road.

"Let's swap," I say.

"Not in that way," she giggles. Her face turns serious, "Now, I know you will keep thinking about every possible thing you could have done to prevent this. But you heard what the doctor said."

"Don't worry, I'll be fine," I force a smile. "I still can't believe you came all the way."

"Well, I had to tick your little district off my bucket list at some point," she closes the door with a grin.

I drag my feet back inside the house to catch some sleep. I've been given two weeks' leave from work, but the doctor told me to let her know if I need more time to get better physically.

I have physical scars.

From riding a bicycle to the hammer mill.

From falling.

From burning myself with hot water because I was too young to cook for my siblings.

From everything else I can't remember.

I nursed them. With herbs, salt, and methylated spirit when it was available. And they all got better. Some are not even visible. Loss, however, I have no idea how to deal with it. I don't know how to nurse what I can't see. How will I even know when it gets better?

Marjory's gentle nudge on my shoulder wakes me up.

"Hey, food is ready."

"What?" I rub my eyes and check my phone. It's 13:26. "Shit, I didn't mean to sleep this long. Sorry, you had to come and cook."

"Oh, forget it. I got permission to leave when I was done with my lessons. Nothing much to do anyway. Grade twelves will be starting their exams soon so it's just revision mostly."

I get out of bed and carry the plate of mince and rice that she came with to the dining table. Eating from the bed is making me feel like a patient.

Chapter 27

When I go back to work, I keep interactions with colleagues to a minimum. I don't want conversations to spill into my personal life. I'm doing a good enough job reminding myself of what I'm going through without anyone's assistance.

Fortunately, there are three more weeks before the next mop-up exercise of the household survey. Until then, I can relax in the office and avoid any field work.

This is also the exact number of weeks to Wezi's return. I shut my eyes and take a deep breath. I haven't yet responded to his message today. Lately, our conversations have been like job interviews.

I pick up my phone from my table and read the message again.

Wezi: Hey. Hope you slept all right. Have a great day at work.

I type the first reply then I delete it.

He didn't call me 'baby' so why should I?

Me: Hey. Thanks, study well.

He said he has exams next week and winding up his thesis. He can have all the space he wants now.

One of my work friends, a physiotherapist, has been transferred to Lusaka. There is a farewell party for him at his house. I'm very reluctant to go. I don't feel like being part of any crowd these days. Marjory succeeds in dragging me out of bed. I don't stress much with my looks. Jeans and a T-shirt will do just fine.

Pretty much everyone I know in the health department circles is there by the time we get to the house. Some other officers too.

Including Patricia.

Neither of us acknowledges the other's presence.

I had initially planned to spend just an hour here tops, but now I'm relieved to be able to pretend that I'm ok. Not even the loud music is bothering me. I'm not taking any alcohol, but the Fanta is still giving me enough motivation to wriggle in my seat to the beat of Yo Maps' song that's now playing.

Wezi calls and I pick up but with the loud music and bad internet reception, I'm forced to cut him off and text. It's weird because he never calls me around this time.

Me: Hey, sorry bad network. I'm still at Mekelani's place.

Wezi: So, when it comes to chatting with me, you're not fine, but you can stay up late at parties?

Me: Seriously?

Wezi: Who are you with?

Me: Who do you think I'm with?

Wezi: Anyway, it's your life after all.

I don't further the conversation. I had already communicated this before leaving the house.

"Hey, are you ok?" Marjory nudges my side with her elbow.

"Yeah," I lie.

"Well, let's get our food before they leave only salads for us," she gets up and leads the way to the braai stand.

We get home a few minutes before 22:00. As soon as I change into my night dress, my phone chimes.

Wezi: Where are you?

I roll my eyes.

Me: Home.

Wezi: Ok. Goodnight.

Me: Goodnight.

◆◆◆

I move the chair that I've been offered towards the big mirror fixed on the wall. The young man standing behind me removes the ribbon and lets my hair fall to my shoulders. He pauses and watches my hair for a minute.

"Madam, why are you cutting such beautiful hair? A lot of women wish they had it," he says.

I shut my eyes and take a deep breath, "Nothing. Just cut it please."

"How much of it?"

"Everything."

He picks up a pair of scissors and chops off chunks of the hair. Then he uses the machine to even it out.

"Should I add a shade? I think it would look good on your type of head. Like this one," he points at a picture of a South African celebrity.

"Ok." I shrug. It doesn't matter who I look like. I just want the hair out of my head.

I walk out of the stuffy room feeling relieved and light. It's as if the heaviness in my heart was being carried on my head.

Marjory looks at me briefly when I walk past her in the sitting room on my way to the bedroom.

The door swings open as soon as I close it.

"I thought I was hallucinating when you walked in. What on earth have you done to your hair?" Her expression is a mixture of bewilderment and exasperation.

"It's just hair," I shrug nonchalantly.

"It's not *just* hair! This is your hair. My goals. Why would you do that to me?"

"Stop being dramatic."

"Typical of people with nice things. So ungrateful," she grunts and turns around to leave.

I prop up my pillows on the bed and lean on one elbow, pouting my lips to take several pictures. I swipe back and forth and choose the best one which I send to Wezi.

Wezi: ??????

Me: What?

Wezi: You look beautiful, but why did you cut it?

Me: I didn't know I needed permission to look the way I want.

We: No baby, I don't mean it like that.

Me: Ok.

Wezi: How was your day?

Me: Fine.

Wezi: Mine was not bad. Just finishing up the paper for submission on Monday. Can't wait to come home next week.

Me: That's nice.

Chapter 28

Wezi called me as soon as he arrived in the district yesterday. I've been in the field for the last three days and going back home today. I should be over the top that he is back.

For good.

Yet the only things that fill my head are questions. Does he still feel the same way about us?

We hadn't discussed the exact time we wanted to get married before the pregnancy.

Maybe it wasn't even him who came up with the idea.

What if he blames me for what happened?

My phone buzzes with several messages when we have a strong network a few kilometres away from the boma.

I open my Whatsapp chats with Wezi, noting the time gap between August and now.

Wezi: Baby let *ba* Katebe drop you guys off at my place. I've cooked lunch.

Me: Ok baby

Mr. Katebe comes inside the house with Marjory and me. After they exchange pleasantries, Wezi hands him a bottle of whiskey and some parcels.

The three of us only have casual conversations while we eat.

"*Mulamu*, thank you for the meal. I have to go now before I fall asleep right here on this sofa," Marjory giggles.

I get to my feet and see her out.

"Hi," Wezi says when I get back in the house. He gets up from his seat, but he doesn't walk towards me.

"Hi," I reply, avoiding his eyes. I put my hands in the back pockets of my jeans and remain standing in my spot.

There has never been so much awkwardness between us.

He should be holding me.

I should be crying in his arms.

None of that happens. We are both waiting for the other to make the first step.

I sit in the corner of one of the sofas. He does the same on the other one.

"How have you been?" he says.

"Good," I shrug. "How did you travel?"

"Bit of turbulence when getting to KK, but nothing unusual."

"Great."

He picks up the remote and starts to flip through the channels, "Want to watch something?"

"No, I'll just bath and take a nap, I'm exhausted."

"Ok," he says.

He remains in his seat while I move around the house.

He remains in his seat while I bath.

He remains in his seat while I nap.

There's no point in me being here. I get up from the bed and follow him to the sitting room. "Hey, I think I'll be leaving now."

I can't make out his exact expression when he looks briefly at me, "I thought you were spending the night?"

"I think it's better if I sleep in my bed. It will be easier to wake up early tomorrow."

"Oh, ok," he gets up and carries my backpack. His phone rings and he spends our entire walk talking to whoever it is on the other end.

Marjory gives me a quizzical look when I get inside the house, but I go straight to my bedroom without saying a word.

◆◆◆

The back and forth between communities in the last two weeks has left me all stressed out. We were supposed to be done before Christmas, but the exercise dragged until halfway into the first week of January.

Wezi travelled for his work meetings and went to visit his family before the New Year holiday. He's been back for a couple of days, yet we have both been dancing around each other.

The other evening, he was at the bar until 21:00. When I passed there on my way to the market after work, Patricia was sitting across from him and several other guys.

He saw me and acted as if it was the most natural thing in the world.

I came to his place this morning and after periods of silence between us, he said he'd be back in a *bit*. I texted him an hour ago that the food is ready, but he is still at the bar with his friends.

This has been his annoying trend ever since he came back last year.

I type another message asking him if I should leave. I'm about to press the send button when his footsteps reach the veranda.

He smells of garlic, which he chews whenever he is drinking. He never drinks to get drunk, but he drinks every time he wants to talk to me these days.

"Hey," he says and slumps on the sofa away from me.

"Hey," I match his boring energy. I flip through some channels, but I can't focus. The frustration that's been taking root in my heart is now consuming all of me. I take deep breaths and count up to sixty.

It's not working.

I switch off the TV and swirl to face him. "Is there something you want to tell me?" My heart is palpitating.

"Like what?"

It's not so much his shrug as it is his nonchalant tone that infuriates me more.

"Like everything! You are here, but you're not even *here*. Sometimes I feel like coming to this house is a waste of time. Do you even want me here?"

He eyes me for a couple of seconds and shakes his head, "If I didn't want you here, I would have told you so. Where's this even coming from?"

"From the fact that you don't want to talk to me!"

"Yeah, how am I supposed to do that? You're always upset about one thing or the other."

"How can you know that I'm upset all the time when you're always avoiding me? You haven't even touched me since you came!"

"Because... you're healing," he gesticulates.

"I healed weeks ago! It was a miscarriage, not an operation."

"So why didn't you just tell me?"

"When have I ever had to *tell* you?"

"I don't know Sanana, these days I'm scared to do anything with you. I'm constantly treading on eggshells and it's exhausting," he huffs.

I scoff, "If I'm that horrible why don't you just leave then!"

"Why are you so quick to say that? Have you found someone else?"

"I'm not cheap like you, Wezi."

"No really, tell me so that I stop wasting my time because you seemed to be doing fine when I was away."

"How dare you even say that? Do you know what I had to endure while you were busy getting your master's whatever and living your best life? I was pregnant. With your child! As if that was not scary enough, I lost the baby. Alone. I cried myself to sleep and woke up from nightmares every single day. Alone."

"It didn't seem like that that when you were out partying."

I'm a bit lost.

"Partying? Have you lost your mind?"

"Are you denying that you went to a party in November?"

I do a quick calculation and then it hits me.

"Let me see your phone," I say, surprised at my own words. I've never done this. *We* have never done this. We've had an unspeakable trust and boundaries around each other's gadgets. He can answer my phone and I his if it's someone we both know and that's it. But it's hard to trust anything between us now.

"Why?"

"What are you hiding?"

"Are you being serious right now?"

"Do you see a joke on my face?" I stretch out my hand.

He clicks his tongue and puts the phone in my palm.

I scroll through the chats, switching from Whatsapp to WeChat. Everyone who cared to communicate with him the whole of last year used this app.

My chat with him is at the top. He still has my number saved as *Suited*. I changed it back to his government name on my phone. Next are his friends, workmates, and his sisters. There are also some names I don't know and the chats are short and mundane.

I keep scrolling.

I will hold this phone until rapture if I have to.

Patricia's name pops up and I open the chat. It starts from the time he just got to China.

February 10, 2021

Patricia: Hi, I heard you left, hope you had a safe trip.

Wezi: I did, thank you. Hope you're fine too

February 14, 2021

Patricia: Happy Valentine's.

Wezi: Thanks, you too.

March 12, 2021

Patricia: Hi

Wezi: Hello

Patricia: How's school?

Wezi: Great. How's work?

Patricia: So so. Anyway, just wanted to say Happy youth day.

Wezi: Thanks. Same.

May 25, 2021

Patricia: Happy birthday to her.

This was a response to the photo he had put on his status on my birthday.

May 26, 2021

Wezi: Thankyou ☺

July 5, 2021

Patricia: Hey you.

Wezi: Hi.

Patricia: How are you?

Wezi: Fine thanks. You?

Patricia: I'm good. How's China?

Wezi: It's all good.

Patricia: Are you coming to vote?

Patricia:?

July 7, 2021

Wezi: Maybe, I'm not sure.

Patricia: Bring me something nice.

August 20, 2021

Patricia: Hi, still around? Haven't seen you since after the elections.

Wezi: No, I already left.

Patricia: You should be saying. Lol

September 13, 2021

Patricia: Looking good as always.

This was a reply to his status. Although the photo is blurred, I remember it. He had sent it to me and I replied with a drooling emoji.

Wezi: Thank you.

October 24, 2021

Patricia: Happy Independence Day.

Wezi: Thank you, Happy Independence Day to you too.

November 20, 2021

Patricia: This same girlfriend of yours is all over the place.

The next message was a picture of me and Mekelani at his farewell party. She had cropped out Richard, Mweemba, and another female workmate. In the original photo, Mekelani was standing between us, hugging us on each side.

What a total bitch!

Wezi had not replied to that text, but that was what must have triggered his attitude that night.

I toss the phone on the cushion next to him and pace the room. "Why the hell do you still have that slut's number?"

"Have you found what you were looking for?"

I let out a sarcastic chuckle, "Don't downplay this Wezi. You knew what she was up to and instead of putting an end to it, you went along like a fool, 'Hi, thanks, you too'," I mimic his texts and click my tongue in disgust.

"There's nothing there that says I'm interested in her because I am not!"

"So, block her!"

He sighs.

"Why can't you? What's so difficult about that?"

"Babe," he reaches for me, but I push his hand away.

"Why?"

"Because … Guys are not like you women."

I stare at him incredulously, "Unless you're keeping her as a backup plan."

"Ok, that's just insulting now."

I fold my arms and cock my head to look him in the eye.

"I can't believe this. Three years," he puts his fingers up. "For *three* years I've done nothing but love you. Even when I was away, I stayed committed to you."

"Oh please, you are not the only one who's put in the work in this relationship, or whatever it is to you,"

"I asked you to marry me."

"Because I was pregnant! Would you have done it otherwise?"

"God, here we go again. I thought we were over that," he rubs his palm against his forehead.

"*You* were over that. As soon as the baby was out of the picture." My voice breaks. I slap away the tears and go to his room. I throw some of my things into an overnight bag. "But you don't have to feel obligated anymore," I say when I come back to the sitting room, bag over my shoulder and a small plastic in hand.

The pregnancy may have been accidental, but I never wanted a marriage of convenience. He only proposed because he felt that was the *right* thing to do given the circumstances. Probably thought I trapped him.

Maybe he's been looking for a way out but just couldn't come clean. I'm not going to wait until he tosses me aside. I'll be the one to end this.

He gets up and stands in the sitting room doorway, "Ok Sanana, what do you want?"

Really?

"Nothing. You are free to be with people you want."

"Wait what?"

"I'm done."

"What's the meaning of all this?"

"I'm just making it easy for you."

He eyes me as I shift my weight between my feet. "You're enjoying this, aren't you? Making up all these scenarios just so you can have your justification. To paint me the bad guy."

I scoff and roll my eyes.

"You should have told me this sooner. There was no point for me to come back here." He steps aside.

I walk out of the door and stop to take a deep breath. The palpitations get faster with every step I take away from him. It's like someone is choking and suffocating and drowning me all at the same time. A part of me expects him to run after me, to apologise and ask me to stay. To tell me he wanted to marry me for me and not the baby. But that only happens on TV.

I'm out of tears by the time I get to my house. I walk past Marjory like a zombie and go straight to my bedroom, locking the door as soon as I step inside. Thankfully, she doesn't knock.

I want to be alone.

◆◆◆

If you are going to try to get over someone, don't listen to sad songs. The only thing it will make you do is cry and remember why you are crying so you can cry some more. I've learnt this after three weeks of playing Adele, Taylor Swift, Sam Smith, and every breakup song that was a hit when it was released.

I have tried to channel my hurt and anger into my work, but it's even more frustrating than just being hurt and angry while doing nothing. If I ever recover from this then I will never again have anything to do with love. Love is stupid. I'll just focus on making money.

I can't talk about this with Marjory because she keeps insisting that Wezi and I are just upset and need to cool down before we discuss things.

I don't want a discussion with Wezi. I want to get over him, soon.

Precious is probably busier with work than I am and she has a backlog of assignments. At least her relationship is going great. I don't want to burden her with my problems. I'm also certain Wezi hasn't told her that we broke up either. She would have called me immediately.

My mother is the last person I want to pour out my emotions to. The only thing that comes second to my parents' entitlement to my money is their eagerness to have an in-law. When I told my mother about the miscarriage, she just told me not to worry because I will have other children. That a lot of women go through the same and get over it. I was in distress and needed her to go through the process with me. But I didn't get that kind of mother. I can't help but question if I could have even trusted my parents around my child.

Wezi has the perfect parents. There's no doubt they'd be there anytime.

Just like every other time, my mind circles back to Wezi. I quickly remind myself of how much he has hurt me so that I summon the right feelings to attach to these unsolicited thoughts.

These thoughts are interrupted by the knock on my door.

Mweemba lets himself in before I answer.

"Since when did we start giving each other surprise visits?" I roll my eyes.

"Just checking if people are in their offices, on behalf of the district commissioner," he smirks.

"Oh please."

He is playing ignorant, but I suspect Wezi has told him what's going on or not going on between us.

"I need to verify something on that report from last week. There's a TB patient who gets packs from the clinic. It seems his wife is also registered in another community." He takes the seat in front of me and flips through the papers on my table.

"Huh, your people also, *awe mwe*. Last time it was that household that kept collecting packs for a child who had been dead for almost a year."

"As I'm talking to you, another family is waiting for me to mediate a feud at the clinic," he chuckles. "The person who collects packs for the patient says they won't be doing it since the patient doesn't share with them."

I pull out the reports folder from the filing cabinet and open the spreadsheet on my laptop. I have to make sure I update any changes we make. "I was even about to do the pie chart summary."

He goes through the list and verifies the details of the beneficiary. I delete the duplicate household from the system.

Chapter 29

N
ews of Mr. Katebe's untimely death
spreads like wildfire. I can't speak or walk
straight on my way out of the office. He
was admitted to the clinic last evening. I was planning to
visit him when I knock off. He had only complained of a
headache when I was with him on Friday and he was being
humorous about it as he drove me home. It turned out he
was hypertensive and had not kept the condition in check.
Although some sections of the community have ruled
otherwise. It's not uncommon for all sorts of theories to pop
up when a deceased is the breadwinner in his family.

The whole district comes to a standstill.

Scores of people from around the town come to
mourn the man; the women he had driven to the hospital
for their deliveries, children whose mothers he had driven to
the hospital over the years, and anyone who saw him drive
the ambulance. Opposing politicians put aside their
differences for his sake. The senior chiefs also come to pay
their respects.

It's the biggest funeral I've witnessed in the years I've
lived here.

All the shops are closed and offices are empty. They
have to move his body from the church to the council hall
for more space, but it doesn't make any difference.

Mr. Katebe was originally from Mansa, but he had worked in Milenge for over fifteen years so the community insisted that he be buried among the people he lived with.

The MP, who is in the district, gives a very compelling send-off message before he breaks down in tears.

Dr. Chisulo is inconsolable and fails to give her speech.

I've never been so gutted by the passing on of someone as much as Mr. Katebe. Not even my blood relatives. It's been three days and I'm still struggling with disbelief. He made work bearable for me. When I was too tired to address people and it was just the two of us, he would chip in. He would translate the difficult words for me. He would calm chaotic situations for me. And even when we got stuck on the road, he would make it feel like a pass time.

If only I had seen him for the last time that morning when I had the chance. But Wezi was there and I didn't want to deal with that.

Marjory and I walk home after helping to clean up at the funeral house. We've both lost our voices and my throat is scratchy from the crying. Most mourners have left and it is just family members left to conduct *isambo lyamfwa*—a common ritual in the north where the family decides what happens with the deceased's property, spouse, and children.

A part of me is curious to know how things will go in Mr. Katebe's case with his two wives.

"This still feels like a dream," Marjory strains herself to speak when we get inside the house. She places the container of *munkoyo* that we carried from the funeral house in the fridge.

"I don't think I will ever recover from this," I clear my throat, hoping that will stop my voice from sounding croaky. It is a futile attempt. I gulp down two glasses of water.

"I'll go and try to get some sleep," she yawns. Neither of us has had enough sleep the last couple of days with work and going to the funeral house.

"Me too."

The knocking on my door wakes me up. "Hey, let's escort Wezi. I don't want to walk back alone," Marjory says, peeking her head through the doorway.

I grudgingly get out of bed and slip into a cotton dress and a pair of sandals. I'm too tired to argue.

Wezi and I have not been on speaking terms since our fight and I've avoided running into him at all costs. I blocked his number and deleted it from my phone. Not that it makes any difference since it's one of the only three numbers I know by heart. We made eye contact a few times during the funeral, although neither of us said a word to the other.

The three of us walk to Wezi's house. He and Marjory make small talk about the funeral and how each of them met the late.

When we reach the front door, Marjory turns to both of us and says, "Well, my work here is done. You two need to sort out your issues. I'm tired of being your middle person."

She doesn't wait for my response before walking away.

I stand with my arms folded across my chest, staring at the ground. Wezi steps forward, unlocks the door, and waits for me to go inside.

Perhaps deep down there's a part of me that only avoided looking at him the last couple of days because seeing him like this breaks my heart. Not just for me. He is hurting and all I want to do is hold him and tell him how much I miss him because I do.

I get inside and sit in the corner of his sofa. I cross my legs and busy myself with my phone as if this is not the house that I'm all too familiar with.

"Hi," he says, taking a seat on the adjacent sofa.

I don't think anyone has ever said that word any slower than he just did.

"Hi," I glance at him briefly and look away. I bite my quivering lower lip and blink hard. I've had too many tears for the day and I am not about to break down again.

"How are you?"

Why does he have to take my hand when he asks that? I didn't see him move close.

"I'm fine." I try to pull back my hand, but he holds it tighter.

"I'm sorry."

"Ok." I still don't look at him. I close and open my eyes and take slow breaths.

He gently takes my phone from my hands and puts it on the table. He kneels in front of me and places his head on my lap. When I don't react, he lifts his head, reaches out his hand, and tilts my chin so that I'm facing him.

"Babe, I'm sorry. For everything," his voice breaks.

My whole body is shaking. I sniff and close my eyes as I lose the fight against my tears. I blow out another slow breath.

He sniffs, "He was like a father to me, you know. That day in Mansa when you were coming from your first workshop … When I called him to confirm about the lift he said, 'Yes, I'm here with your madam'. He referred to you as my 'wife' since that day at the junction," he chuckles softly, ignoring the tears that are cascading down his cheeks. "He knew even when I didn't. He saw everything I was too naive to notice. He was always there when I needed to talk to him about some things I was conflicted with. Even back in China, when these people tried to fill me with doubts, he always said, 'That one is not like that, don't mess it up'.

Now I messed it up and… he's gone," he buries his face in my lap and cries.

I lift my trembling hand and caress his head. I can't bear to see him like this.

While I interacted with Mr. Katebe on a more professional level, Wezi had a personal relationship with and looked up to him as a bonafide friend and mentor. Most of the people he hangs out with are his age mates, but he and Mr. Katebe spent a significant amount of time together. I can't think of a time that Wezi came from a trip without buying the older man a bottle of Grants or Jack Daniels. He never did that for anyone else.

I cry for his loss. I can't even imagine what he is going through.

"I don't know how else to fix this but I'm sorry. I should have been more understanding of what you went through when I wasn't around to help you deal with it," he says.

I cup his head and press my forehead against his.

"I'm sorry too," I sob.

He puts his arms around my waist and holds me as if he's afraid I will slip away.

We stay like this for a long time.

When he is calm, he slowly gets up and takes my hands in his. He hugs me again when we are both standing. "Please stay with me tonight. I just want to hold you. You are the only one I want to be with right now." He lets go and squeezes his eyes with his thumb and index finger. "But if you don't want to—"

"I'll stay," I stop him. "I'll stay. Tonight... and tomorrow, and the day after."

He chuckles and hugs me again, "I love you."

"I love you too."

◆◆◆

I wake up to the smell of fried eggs and grilled sausage.

Wezi places the tray of food on one side of the bed. He stabs a chip with the fork and puts it in my mouth.

I sit up to make room for him.

"I thought you would make me those *tuma* nice noodles," I giggle. My voice is worse than it was yesterday. I need to find some Lozenges later.

"I thought you prefer this for breakfast."

"Well, there's always room for change."

He clears his throat, "Speaking of change, I uhm, got my promotion."

I put down the piece of sausage I was about to put in my mouth. This is huge.

"Baby?"

"The former Provincial Works Supervisor was appointed as PS for our ministry. My immediate supervisor was promoted to that position and now me. I got the letter last week when I went to Mansa."

"Wait, you got the letter last week? Why didn't you tell me?"

He raises an eyebrow.

"Oh," I say, lowering my eyes sheepishly. "This is great news. Congratulations *ba* senior provincial works supervisor."

"Thanks."

I jump out of bed on a whim, "We need to celebrate!"

"Hmm, no. I don't want to publicise it," he shakes his head. "You are the first person I'm telling and I'd like to keep it that way until I do my handovers with the district commissioner."

I sigh and crawl back into bed. "You're right. What am I even thinking? You're leaving. Which also means, *you're leaving*."

The reality of the situation hits me like a giant rock. Shit.

"It's just Mansa, babe," he cups my face and kisses my forehead.

I curl up against him, "Am I a bad person for hating this situation?"

"No. I hate it too. But we will make it work, I promise."

It is a strange feeling to be happy and sad in the same breath.

"When I lost the baby—"

"When *we* lost the baby," he corrects me.

"I thought you were angry with me."

"Why would you think that?"

I shrug, "You sounded upset and distant all the time. You never asked for pictures of me anymore and… and—"

"Come on babe. It wasn't your fault. And I was angry, but it was at the circumstances. I never blamed you for what happened. I couldn't even be here for you, and then the exams. I don't know how you had to deal with all that on your own. And when I got here it was like you had started moving on without me."

Tell that to this heart that has a life of its own.

"I missed you," I kiss him.

"I know, you said it a hundred times last night," he smirks.

"I'm leaving." I roll out of bed, but he pulls me back.

"No, you're not, I haven't finished making it up to you."

I straddle him and he kisses me.

Chapter 30

I'm travelling with Wezi to Mansa. He has left all his things for me to sell and keep whatever I want. The divan bed is my favourite of them all. Followed by the Addis storage box which I've been using whenever I travel out of the district. It's very handy for all grocery shopping.

He insisted that I go with him to pick out the new bed and all the necessary household items that he needs for the new house. Musenge helped him find a neat two-bedroomed flat.

"Road trip number what?" he asks.

"I've even lost count," I smile. "Because unfortunately, you are now just some guy who's inside my heart."

"Oh really?"

"Yeah, somewhere between the two ventricles."

"I wonder where I'll be when we take our first flight together."

"That's when you'll become my soulmate."

"So, you do have a soul," he grins.

I scowl at him.

"What are you going to miss the most about this place?" I take his hand in mine.

He is pensive for a moment then says, "The day I arrived at the junction. I remained in my seat because I thought the bus had missed my stop. So, the conductor went like '*this* is Milenge'. I was directly facing him in my seat. I looked out of the window and back at him before I stood up.

"And when my luggage was out, I just stood there staring at my surrounding. The bus had carried some supplies for the hospital. When the boys had finished loading the boxes in the ambulance, Mr. Katebe looked at me and said, 'Young man, if you need a lift to the boma, jump in, you can continue crying when you get there'. And when we got to the boma, he went with me to his house to eat and helped me get a room at a guest house. A couple of days later, he rented me one of his flats, the one you and Marjory live in now. That's where I stayed until I moved to the complex."

He takes a deep breath and lets out a soft chuckle, "So that day we met you, he said it wasn't a coincidence."

I rest my head on his shoulder and close my eyes.

◆◆◆

"We will see how she survives now that the *ka* boyfriend has left," one of the hospital cleaners says to her colleague. She has her back to me as she mops the passage near one of the side rooms. "She thought she was all that just because she was going out with an engineer."

They probably assumed I'd gone in the field since I left with my backpack earlier.

"Hmm, *bana* Chali," the friend replies. "Sanana doesn't have a problem with anyone, she just minds her business. *Elo* from the time I knew Wezi, I never saw him with anyone until she came. He loves that girl. Imagine someone going abroad and coming back for you. How many Zambian men can do that? Sometimes just be happy for other people."

"Stop defending her just because she gives you *tuma* things."

"She also gives you things."

"Yes, but I'm not going to worship her just because she does. After all, she gets paid a lot of money for just gallivanting."

I don't bother to excuse myself. I drag my feet all over the floor she has just mopped and unlock my office door.

◆◆◆

I kick off my gumboots in the kitchen. Marjory is in the sitting room with a girl plaiting her hair.

"You're back early today?" she says.

"We didn't find the community members at one of the points so we just did two and were done by lunchtime. Now I have to go back on Monday, aargh." I walk to where she is seated on the floor and inspect her cornrows. "These are neat. Where did you find this one?"

"She's in my class. I found her plaiting her friend's hair during prep. This is her punishment."

The girl giggles.

"How much do you charge? I think this will be a better alternative to the braids I wanted, it gets too hot in the field."

My hair has grown a sizeable length for plaiting in the last five months since I cut it. I thought shorter hair was easier to maintain, but I was very mistaken.

The girl hesitates.

"Don't worry, she'll do it for free," Marjory says.

"Hmm madam," the girl starts, but Marjory cuts her off.

"It's an extension of your punishment. Consider it experience for your future salon business since it seems more important than your education," she laughs.

"Madam it's not fair."

"After all you ate my Nshima."

"But I cooked," the girl giggles.

"It wasn't your mealie meal."

"*Mwandini* madam it's K10," she finally says to me. "I can come and do it tomorrow after church."

"That will work just fine," I say.

I drag my feet to the bedroom and collapse on the bed. This is when my weekend is starting.

◆◆◆

Mweemba picks me up from my house around 10:00. I had wanted to leave home early, but Wezi would not have it. He insisted that I get enough rest for the day ahead.

He has been in Mansa for almost three months. I haven't seen him in two weeks and I'm dying to spend my birthday with him. I should have gotten used to the long-distance thing by now. Especially that, unlike China, either of us commutes between the two towns whenever we are free. Still, missing him gets worse every day.

We've been planning my birthday trip to Samfya since the beginning of the month and to that effect, we have each taken some days off work. We will leave Samfya tomorrow and spend the weekend in Mansa.

Marjory travelled to Luanshya for a family programme yesterday. I asked Precious if she would be in Samfya today, but she said she will be commemorating Africa Freedom Day in Lunga with the rest of the district staff. She will only be back tomorrow.

I'd have loved for both my friends to be present for my birthday. I guess it will have to be just me and Wezi. Not that I'm complaining. We haven't had a romantic getaway in a while. And I finally get to go to Samfya just for the beauty of it.

We meet Wezi at Kwacha Waterfront. Mweemba says something about visiting some relatives and leaves.

"I missed you," he pulls me in a tight hug and brushes his lips against mine. After all these years, I still get butterflies in my stomach when he does this.

"And you smell nice," I kiss him back.

"But I always wear this perfume."

"Huh, maybe this bottle is original," I giggle.

He chuckles, "Maybe your nostrils get clogged in the village."

"Hmm, it has become a village now *ka*. Traitor."

He takes my hand and leads me to the luxurious room he's booked. It is directly facing the lake.

He lets me sleep for a couple of hours and when I wake up, he hands me a gift box. I open it excitedly. Inside is the emerald green maxi dress from Fab Galore boutique. I had mentioned Precious and Marjory under one of their Facebook posts.

"Baby, I love it! Thank you," I throw my arms around his neck and pull him back to the bed.

"As much as I would love to do this, we have to go," he smiles, rolling off the bed.

"Go where?"

"There's a boat cruise waiting for us."

I squeal and jump out of bed, "Why didn't you tell me?"

"I just did," he beams.

He helps me get into the dress.

I pull a chair from the study table and drag it to the dressing table in front of a large mirror.

"Why do you always hide that?" he watches me cover my birthmark with concealer.

"It doesn't look nice," I shrug.

He bends over, cups my face and kisses the mark under my eye. "It's my favourite part of your face."

"Oh please."

"I'm serious. *Flawlessness*, as you people call it, is overrated. I can't even hug and kiss you properly with all the powder on your face. And I will be kissing you a lot tonight," he winks.

"Fine." I turn back to the dressing mirror and start wiping my face. "But the lashes and lipstick are remaining."

He changes into a polo T-shirt and a pair of cotton pants.

We take a taxi to Samfya Marines.

He covers my face with a blindfold when we get out of the car.

"This is how people get killed," I giggle as he leads me down the stairs to the beach.

"At least in your case, it would be by the love of your life."

"You wish."

We stop when I start to feel the sand in my sandals and he goes behind me to take off the blindfold.

"Surprise!" the whole bunch choruses before I fully take their faces in.

I look at Wezi who has the biggest grin I've ever seen on his face then back to the lake.

Precious, Musenge, Mweemba, Kahilu and his girlfriend, and Marjory are all on board the Samfya Marines speed boat. The boat is decorated with balloons and some rose petals sprinkled all over. All of them are holding out happy birthday posters and wearing party hats.

"I'm not going to cry," I say, shaking my head. I bring my hands to my face, tears already on my lips. "I'm not going to cry."

Wezi puts his arm around me and squeezes my shoulder, "Happy birthday babe."

"I love you," I say.

He helps me get on the boat and I punch my brother in the gut for being part of the plan.

"You really don't know me if you thought I was gonna miss your birthday for some freedom fighter celebrations," Precious laughs, throwing her arms around me.

"Judas," I say to Marjory.

"Technically, this is a family programme," she grins.

Happy does not even begin to describe how I'm feeling right now.

The boat sets off and Marjory passes drinks around. It's all laughter and fun as we sail away from Samfya

Marines. We meet the big boat cruising in our direction at Chita and exchange waves and screams with the people on it.

We are taking turns with pictures and pretending to sail the boat when Wezi comes in front of me in the aisle and gets on one knee.

Precious alerts everyone to turn around and switch off the music.

"Babe," Wezi says. The guys start whistling, but stop when he clears his throat. "Sanana," he takes a deep breath. "I know that last time it was rushed and you felt like I was doing it out of obligation. The truth is that I wanted to ask you to marry me. Even before I left for school. I just didn't want you to think I was asking you to marry me so that you would be bound to a promise you might not want to keep." He is looking at me and my eyes are blinking back tears. "I want you to be my wife with or without a baby between us. I choose you even if I have to see you only on weekends and public holidays. It's you. It has been from the minute I stood next to you on the side of the road that day."

He goes quiet and just stares at me for a few seconds.

"The question," Precious whispers, sending everyone into laughter.

"Right," he chuckles. "Babe, will you marry me?"

I get on my knees and give him my hand. "Of course, I'm the love of your life."

He laughs as he slips the ring on my finger. He helps me up and wipes my eyes with his thumbs. Everyone is ululating and whistling. He hugs me and kisses my forehead.

"Well, it's a good thing I carried this champagne," Musenge announces, patting Wezi on the back. "This guy was supposed to propose later. It seems he got impatient."

Wezi looks at me and shrugs.

I couldn't have wished for a better moment or place.

We get off the boat at Kwacha waterfront where I'm told everyone is booked for the night.

There's a table reserved for us in the dining room, set with drinks and food. We all get seated and a waiter brings my birthday cake.

When they ask me to make a wish, I just say a silent prayer of thanks.

I am already living my wish, with all these amazing people in it.

Mweemba goes back to Milenge in the morning. The seven of us drive to Mansa together in Musenge's Prado. Kahilu and his girlfriend stay with me and Wezi while Marjory goes to a friend of hers.

"She is even prettier in person," I say to my brother when we get to the Mansa bus station. We will use the same bus going to Lusaka. "How did you get so lucky? I mean look at your nose."

"Look who's talking. Has Wezi seen your feet or do you hide them in socks?"

I stick my tongue out at him. "Just don't get someone's child pregnant before you finish school."

"And take her where?" He laughs. "To your mother's house to eat *litapi*? Does your fiancé know that your family is toxic?"

"Well, he likes you so maybe he's into toxic families."

We get on the bus as soon as our bags are secured in the boot. Kahilu and his girlfriend take the double seats behind me and Marjory.

Marjory stares out of the window, "I hate the trips back to that place. Now I have to keep hiding my WhatsApp statuses from those witches I work with to avoid silly questions," she giggles. "I told my workmates that I had gone to submit something to the provincial education office. After all, I don't owe them explanations. I'm only answerable to the headmaster, who wasn't even around at the time."

She is now the head of the sciences department. Her former supervisor was promoted to another school as deputy headteacher.

Mweemba is already at Milenge junction when we arrive. I bid my brother and his girlfriend farewell. We used the mid-morning bus so they'll probably be in Lusaka after dark.

Marjory and Mweemba are cordial around each other these days, although I'm the one who does most of the talking to either of them on the drive to the boma.

Chapter 31

A hundred reports are waiting for me when I get to the office on Monday. I also have to reconcile the distribution lists for the nutritional packs that I pretended not to have seen before I left last week.

I'll keep a low profile for the coming weeks to avoid attention and unnecessary questions about my engagement. It's enough that I've been getting congratulatory text messages from people who are not even in my friendship circle.

Richard calls me to go over the statistics that have just come in from some of the health posts. I'm jumping on any opportunity to keep my mind off Wezi.

I join the rest of the section heads for a meeting in the boardroom. Each one of us is required to give an end-of-quarter presentation.

I cut the call as soon as my phone makes a sound and push it aside. I'm about to deliver my presentation. It starts to ring again and this time, Dr. Chisulo shoots me a look of irritation. I grab the phone and put it on mute.

My mother only calls when she needs something. I have an idea of what this particular persistence is about. I switch off the phone and shove it in my bag under the table. It's not rocket science that if you call someone twice during working hours and they cut you off then it means they are busy.

I get to the front of the room and give my presentation, making sure to provide all clarity and not have to be asked what I've already addressed. I don't get back to my mother throughout the day. Talking to her will just drain me. I only have the energy to organise my reports. I'll deal with my personal issues when I get home.

It looks like I wasn't the only one waiting for me to get home because my mother calls again as soon as my feet hit the doorstep. The next ten minutes are spent with her expressing her disappointment in me for *letting* my father go to jail because I didn't pick up her calls.

Nothing that my parents do surprises me anymore. It's always one thing or the other. I have built enough immunity against any sort of emotional blackmail. It hasn't been easy, but the older I grow, the more I realise that I can be a good person without bending over backward to prove it.

This time around, my father had involved himself in a fertilizer scam. He and a group of friends had collected money from some other farmers under the pretext that they would get them subsidised farming inputs if they paid a certain amount before the onset of the farming season. He and his three co-accused were sentenced to two years of imprisonment this morning. This was not the first time my father had found himself on the other side of the law and the magistrate was more than eager to send him to the recently constructed Mongu prison.

My mother believes that a bribe would have solved this problem, but who would one bribe to throw away a district scandal involving a hundred-thousand Kwacha?

Not even uncle Masiliso had been interested in showing up to the court hearing.

I put my bag on the floor and crawl onto the bed. I lie there quietly to process everything my mother said. It's no use crying over her negative words. I slap the tears away and text Wezi.

Me: Baby

Wezi: Yes love.

Me: Are you home?

Wezi: Not yet. In a meeting, but will be done soon. Whatsup?

Me: Dad is in jail.

Wezi: How, what happened????

Me: It's a long story, I don't even know where to start.

Wezi: I'll call you as soon as I'm out, ok babe?

Me: All right.

Although I was famished when I left work, I neither have the energy to cook nor the appetite to eat when Marjory brings the food.

"I hope you are not beating yourself up about this," she says, taking a seat on the bed. "Everyone makes their own choices in life and some choices have more grave consequences than others. There is nothing you could have done."

"I don't know *mwe*," I sniff.

"Look, no one is perfect, and that includes parents. We don't choose where we come from and trust me, you're not the only one from a dysfunctional home. My young brother was recently arrested for battering his wife yet she was the one who went to beg for him to be released from police custody. And that wasn't even the first time he did it. I don't feel sorry for her anymore. I've told her countless times to leave the fool, yet she won't listen.

"So, if you want my advice, just eat my friend. The food won't solve these problems, but at least you will have the energy to cry," she grins.

I chuckle and take the plate from her, "You're crazy."

◆◆◆

I've had five malnourished babies put on emergency feeding in the last two hours. I finally have a moment to hide in my office and eat the cornflakes I carried for breakfast.

Shoving my empty lunch box aside, I swipe my phone which has been abandoned for some time on my table.

Precious texted me that the nutritionist under Mansa district resigned to join an NGO.

Me: Are you sure?

Precious: 100%. Musenge heard it from the district health director for Mansa.

Me: And you don't want to move?

Precious: Eww that's like working in the same office with your man.

Precious: And between us, Musenge is not renewing his contract next year. There's another position he was assured of in Lusaka.

Me: Wow! That's great. For him, I mean. *Eish,* just this Mansa distance is frustrating, now what more Lusaka?

Precious: Hahaha all sorted. I want to go on study leave next June for my master's.

Me: Masters *ka,* our friends.

Precious: I just want to get it out of the way. *Elo,* I'm keeping all these books and modules for you.

Precious: So call the provincial office for consideration of the transfer.

Me: Now what about the project? You know these allowances have been my salvation.

Precious: *Iwe,* do something for yourself for once.

Precious: Anyway, Musenge says there are considerations to roll out the project to other districts after the evaluation. It's better you are already that side by then. Before people send their relatives.

Me: *Apa* so I'm even walking to Dr. Chisulo's office. Lol

Precious: Lol.

I'm proud of how far she has come academically. Everyone close to me has progressed in one way or another while my diploma is the only thing I can boast of.

The notion of rural areas being the best places for personal development has not worked for me. These things all depend on where you come from.

Dr. Chisulo was busy when I requested to talk to her yesterday. She called me to her office this morning.

"Are you sure this is what you want?" she gives me a look of concern when I make my transfer request.

"Yes doc," I say, staring at my clasped hands.

"And you are not doing it for your boyfriend or is it fiancé now?"

I smile shyly. She had been among the first people to congratulate me on my engagement.

"You know that there is no project in Mansa, right?" she says.

"Yes doc, I'm aware."

"And you still want to go?"

I nod.

She sighs, "Well, if you have made up your mind, I can't hold you back. You just have to make sure that everything is in order before you leave. Someone will probably leap at the opportunity to come here soon. I will call the Provincial Medical Officer and let him know."

"Thank you, doc."

"When am I receiving my card by the way? You want to just send us pictures of your honeymoon?" she smiles.

I laugh, "Soon. We haven't concluded on the date yet."

"Good luck with the preparations."

"Thank you very much."

I leave her office with a grin that lasts all the way to the hospital and dial Wezi's number.

Epilogue

"Babes," Precious says. "Let us know if you want to cry out here the whole day or if you want to go in there and marry that guy."

"*Elo* you know Wezi, he will just follow us here if we stay out any longer," Marjory adds.

I've been sitting in the car outside The Urban Hotel Ndola for the last thirty minutes. The makeup artist keeps fixing and refixing my makeup because the tears just won't stop coming.

All the guests are already seated in the smaller conference room that we are using for the marriage blessing. We opted that both church service and reception be held here so that we don't waste time on movements between two different venues.

The photography will also be done here.

I got my transfer to Mansa five months ago and have been busy with marriage preparations ever since. Precious and Marjory were on hand, virtually. We only met to finalise all arrangements and details last week.

Wezi's parents paid for the venue as a wedding gift to us.

Last month, I made my first trip to Mongu in four years. I took time to visit my father in jail. He didn't seem remorseful his actions.

My mother, who still holds a grudge against me came to the wedding with some close relatives.

Eta, my third bridesmaid, is standing outside the conference room to signal that we are almost ready. She was given a full scholarship and is almost done with her first year. She whispers something to Mrs. Mushili and the older woman comes over to the car. I asked her to be my matron.

"Sweetheart. It's ok to feel all sorts of emotions. However, you are the reason everyone is gathered in there and until you show up, nothing will happen. So come on, let's get you in there before Wezi thinks you have run away."

"We were just telling her that," Precious giggles.

Mrs. Mushili holds my hand and helps me step out of the car while Precious and Marjory fix and hold the train of my Glynview ball gown wedding dress.

Uncle Masiliso takes my hand at the entrance of the room and smiles at me. He is now the Principal Education Standards Officer for the North-Western province.

I chuckle when *Suited* starts playing.

Memories of the last four years fill my head with every step I take towards Wezi.

It feels like a lifetime since I stood at the junction, scared and wondering what would become of my life.

I'm a little scared. But this time, no part of me wants to jump back on the bus.

END

www.ingramcontent.com/pod-product-compliance
Lightning Source LLC
Chambersburg PA
CBHW020311200626
46814CB00006BA/2188